TO BE LOVED

Lighthouse Lovers
Book 3

SHANNON O'CONNOR

Copyright © 2024 Shannon O'Connor
All rights reserved.

All rights reserved. No part of this publication may be reproduced, distributed, or transmitted in any form or by any means, except in the case of brief quotations embodied in critical reviews and articles.

No use of AI was used to create this book, cover or edit any of the following. Please do NOT use my words, cover, or anything from this book in an AI form to feed AI.

Any resemblance to persons alive or dead is purely coincidental.

Cover by PagesandAdventures.

Edited by Victoria Ellis of *Cruel Ink Editing & Design*.

Proofread by *Cruel Ink Editing & Design*.

Formatted by Shannon O'Connor.

❀ Created with Vellum

To Be Loved Playlist

Hold On - Chord Overstreet

Say OK - Vanessa Hudgens

Lonely Road - mgk, Jelly Roll

Fine by Me - Andy Grammer

IDK How To Talk To Girls - Beth McCarthy

Slow - Andy Grammer

For The Lover That I Lost - Celine Dion

La Vie En Rose - Emily Watts

The Night We Met - Lord Huron

POV - Jason Derulo

BRAINWASHED - Waterparks

Slow Low - Jason Derulo

Bad Ideas - Tessa Violet

Slow Cooker - John Legend

From the Jump - James Arthur & Kelly Clarkson

Out of My League - Aidan Bissett

LET YOU BE RIGHT - Meghan Trainor

Content Warnings

Please note some of these might be considered spoilers for parts of the story.

- Grief/Loss of a spouse
(on page)
- Grief/Loss of parents
(Brief; past mention- not on page)
- Depression
(Past - brief mention)
- IVF; In vitro fertilization
(On page descriptions)
- Pregnancy
(On page descriptions)

ONE

Norah

"How are you doing?" Alana asks with a soft tone. "I'm okay," I say, although I know no matter how many times I say it, she won't believe me.

"Are you sure?" she asks again, like always.

"There are good and bad days, today's a good day," I say.

I don't blame her. I'm not *okay*, but that is a new normal I'm getting used to. I mean, how should I act after the death of my husband? It's been over a year now, and it's still hard to believe it some days. I can't blame my best friend for checking in on me.

"I'm glad it's a good day. I was hoping to ask you a favor." She's on the phone, but I can picture her eyebrows crashing together in stress.

"What's up?"

"Gemma, my friend from college, is coming to stay for the summer. She's my maid of honor and needs a place to stay. I was going to have her stay at the other house on the estate, but there's water damage. Would you be okay with having a roommate?"

"Oh my goodness, of course." I laugh. "It's your family's house after all, don't even worry about it. This place is huge."

"Perfect. I thought about asking Heather, but I know she's not as much of a people person as you are."

"No worries, having a roommate could be fun. Don't even stress," I reassure her.

I've been living at her family's summer house on the Lovers Estate for the last several months. Ever since I sold the house Finn and I lived in, I needed someplace to stay. There are just too many memories of our life together there, and living there without him doesn't make sense. So, until I figure out my next move, I'm living on the estate. I have enough money to rent something, but it's a matter of figuring out if I want to stay in Lovers or if I'll be looking for a house or an apartment.

Alana hangs up, and I grab my book off the counter in the kitchen. If I'm going to have a roommate, I need to tidy up a bit. I'm not messy, but there is definitely *stuff* everywhere. I've made myself at home, and I could afford to clean up after myself. Glancing at my Apple watch, I realize I have another hour before I need to get ready for work. I decide to quickly clean up and make a mental note to vacuum later in the week. Alana said she'd shoot me a text later with more details. I'm actually kind of excited; I haven't lived with anyone since Finn, and I'm definitely a people person.

That's part of the reason I work at the local bookstore, To Be Loved. Being around people and books are my two favorite things. My coworkers are lovely, and so are the people who visit the store. We rarely have a grumpy customer in the bookstore. I know most of the repeat customers since it's a small town. I love giving book recommendations and spending my days talking about books.

Life is a little lonely without Finn. We had our entire lives planned out together, and now he's just...*gone*. Maybe having a roommate won't magically fix that, but it could help with the loneliness.

I get dressed for work in a simple green sundress and a cardigan. Then, I slide on flats and tie some of my red hair back with a clip. I grab the book I'm currently reading and my keys. I pull up to the store five minutes before noon and park in my usual spot in the back. Once I reach the store, the familiar noise of the bells chiming make me smile as I open the door. Sutton, my coworker, looks up from behind the desk where she's helping a customer. She smiles at me briefly while I head to the office to drop off my stuff. I clock in on the antique machine that surprisingly never gets my punches wrong. Then I look at the stock of books that need to be sorted and returned to their spots.

"Hey! How are you?" Sutton smiles, appearing behind me. She's small and quiet so she has a tendency to sneak up on me.

"I'm good. Any trouble today?"

"Nope, just the usuals," she assures me. She's worked here for the last year, a little longer than I have. But because of my experience and my library science degree, I'm technically her boss.

"I'm going to head next door to grab my lunch. Want a coffee?"

"No, but could you grab me a decaf tea? Whichever flavor they have is fine," I say.

"Yup, I'll be back in a few." Sutton takes off her name tag and lets down her light red hair. It's similar to mine, so similar that we often get mistaken for each other.

While she heads next door, I grab a stack of books, put them on the table behind the registers, and wait for a customer. I've noticed a few people in the store that are browsing, and I don't want to be busy if they need help. So I wait for someone to ask me a question or need help finding a book. I tidy up the register area, cleaning with the special spray. It smells stronger than usual today, but maybe it's a fresh batch. We usually pour it from a bigger container in the back.

"Here you are." Sutton returns with a hot cup of tea and disappears into the break room with her lunch.

I open the lid, trying to determine which flavor it is. But as soon as I open the cup I'm hit with a huge whiff of raspberries. I close the lid and take a sip. It tastes good, but it smells extra strong. Maybe I should've asked her to add some milk. I wonder if we have any in the break room...

"Can I check out here?" an older man asks.

"Of course." I smile. He puts down his two books, both on the Civil War.

"Do you need a bookmark?" I ask.

"I'd love one." He smiles.

I grab two free bookmarks from the cup next to me and slide one in each book's title page. I scan the books and take the crumpled-up twenties from him. After handing him his change, I grab a paper bag and slide each book carefully inside.

"Have a nice day." I grin, handing him his bag.

"You too, Norah," he adds with a wink.

Sutton returns from her break and takes over the register while I grab the stack of books I set aside and start sorting. My day is a lot of busy work like this, but I enjoy it. It makes the time pass quickly, and at least I'm not sitting at home crying any longer. The first several months were rough. It seemed like any time I thought I was having a normal day, something would ruin it. I was depressed, and I knew I needed a change. I didn't want to live like that. I knew Finn didn't want me living like that.

So when I moved into the house, getting a job seemed like a good idea. This one is a step down from my last job, and it's only part time. But it's something to keep my mind busy and my stress levels low—two things that are important to me.

"Excuse me, miss? Can you help me?" a tall, blond man asks. I can't help but notice the grin he flashes me; his teeth are bright white and perfect.

"Sure, what can I do for you?" I put down the last of the books I am carrying and walk over to him.

"I'm looking for this set of books, but I see you only have the first two. Would it be possible to order the rest?" He shows me the books on his phone, and I nod.

"Yup! The last two are the newest, and we can never keep

them on the shelf. I'll have you fill out a form, and I can help you order them." I smile. I lead him to the registers because there's a computer for this purpose. I hand him a form to fill out and a pen.

He leans on the counter, flexing his arm muscles against his cotton white T-shirt. I can't tell if he's doing it on purpose or not. When he's done filling out the form, he smiles and hands it back to me.

"I didn't see an option to ship it to the store. Is that not something you do?"

"We do it on an as needed basis. We don't have the capacity to hold hundreds of orders, so we have to check prior to ordering. But for just two books we definitely can."

"Awesome." He flashes me a smile.

"Do you have an ID?"

"I do, but I just moved to town. Does it need to match my address on the form?"

"Nope, just as long as your name is the same." I glance at the form and his ID, seeing his name matches—Elliot Lewis. He moved from Texas. That's quite a jump.

"I know what you're thinking, but I swear...not everyone who lives in Texas is a Republican."

"I didn't say a word. I was just surprised. It seems like a rather far move."

"It was, but I needed a fresh start." He smiles. "Have you lived here long?"

"All my life," I say proudly. I'm a small-town woman at heart.

"Maybe you could show me around some time? I'd love to get to know some of the locals."

"Like a date?" I clarify.

"Yes." He nods.

"No, thank you." I smile tightly. It isn't the first time I've been hit on at work, but it never makes it any easier—or less awkward.

"Oh. Do you have a boyfriend?"

"No. I'm just not dating right now." I wish he wasn't pushing me like this. *No* should suffice. I type the last lines of his responses into the computer and print out a receipt.

"You can pay when you pick up the books. We'll call and email to let you know when they come in, and you have one week to purchase them," I explain as I hand him the receipt.

"Okay. Thanks." I can tell I've shaken his confidence. He doesn't seem like the kind of guy who hears the word *no* very often. He disappears out of the shop, and Sutton rushes to my side.

"Did I hear he asked you out?"

"Yeah." I nod.

"Did you say yes?"

"No. You know I'm not dating right now."

"It's too bad; he's yummy." She winks.

"He was okay, but it's not like I'm even looking right now." I shrug. Sutton nods and I get back to work.

The thought of dating anyone again makes my stomach churn. It almost feels like I'm cheating on Finn. I know I'm not, and I know he's gone. But being with anyone else besides him... I just can't even imagine it. I barely notice men anymore...*like that* anyway. Elliot is handsome, but it doesn't do anything for me. No butterflies in my stomach or alarms going off in my head. Not like when I first met Finn.

He was all butterflies and feeling weak in the knees. Finn was kind of nerdy with dark, round glasses and messy dark curls on his head. But the moment he laid eyes on me, everything stopped. I think that was why I didn't bother looking at anyone else. There was no way anyone could compete with how Finn made me feel. And I never wanted to replace or lose that feeling either. So maybe I'm barely thirty and closing up shop, but it has to be better than the alternative. I can't bring Finn back from the dead, and no other person will ever compare.

TWO

Gemma

"I'm so happy you're here! Was your drive okay?" Alana asks, wrapping her arms around me.

"Yes! Straight through until town just like you said." I smile.

I unlock my trunk and grab my suitcase while Alana grabs the other one. I'm a light packer. I don't need too much, and I'm used to traveling. I'm a nurse, but due to the lack of nurses right now, I'm constantly on the move. I make way more money working short amounts of time at a random place than I do settling down in one spot—which is how I've ended up in Lovers, Maine. Well, one of the reasons. The other being that I'm Alana's maid of honor and I need to make sure this wedding goes off without a hitch.

The house is freaking huge, and we passed three other similar looking ones on the property. This house is a light blue color with white shutters and a dark green door. There's a huge front yard and flowers everywhere. I wonder if someone is hired to take care of them or if it's something my new roomie does.

"Norah, my friend and your new roomie, is at work. But she said to make yourself at home and help yourself to anything in the fridge. I think she even baked cookies."

"Shit, I knew you said she was nice, but damn." I'm impressed. I've never had a stranger bake me cookies.

"She's a sweetheart. But she's going through a bit of a rough patch since her husband passed away suddenly last year."

"Oh crap." My face falls.

"Yeah. I just figured I'd mention it. She doesn't talk about it too much, but I thought you should know."

"Make sure I don't make any stupid jokes—got it."

"When do you start work?" she asks, changing the subject.

"On Monday. I report to Lovers General Hospital for my first twelve-hour shift there."

"Got it. I don't know how you do it. I'm tired after working from home, and you're working on your feet for twelve hours."

"You get used to it." I shrug. It isn't so bad. Once I get the hang of how things are run, I'm usually moving on to the next place that needs me. It isn't like I have much time to form attachments.

"Norah's room is over here, so this is your room."

Alana leads me down a white hallway and into a deep purple room. The furniture is all white with small purple accents. I'm more impressed with how big this place is and the fact that it's only a guest place for Alana's family. We were roommates in college, so I've always known she's rich. But to see it like this is impressive. She'd always invited me to come visit for the summer, but I thought I'd be imposing so I never took her up on it. Now I'm kicking myself for it.

"This is honestly too much. I can stay in a hotel."

"Nonsense, you're here for my wedding. The least I can do is provide you with free housing." Alana waves me away.

"I signed a contract to stay until the end of September, is that okay?"

"Of course. *Mi casa es su casa.*" Alana smiles.

"You know we both failed freshman Spanish because we were too hungover to go to class."

"What's mine is yours," she clarifies.

"Ah." I nod.

"How's the fiancé? He didn't want to come help me move in?" I tease.

Will and I have never really got along. It's probably something I need to let go of at this point, but I don't know how. It isn't that he *did* anything, but we just rub each other the wrong way. I think Alana can do better than him, and I'm pretty sure he's picked up on that. Alana used to have so much drive, and it seems like she's just settling for Will. I only brought this up once at the beginning of their relationship. Of course, only because Alana asked for my honest opinion. She disagreed, and I noticed that she never asked me about him again. I've kept my mouth shut ever since.

"He had a big meeting today; he's actually in New York for it." Her mouth forms a line.

"All good otherwise?" I'm poking, but isn't that the job of the maid of honor? If she's going to pull a runaway bride, I need to be prepared to drive the getaway car.

"Oh yeah. Just pre-wedding jitters." She waves me off again, and I nod. I can take a hint. This isn't something she wants to talk about with me.

"Do you want to grab some lunch?" I ask.

"I'd love to, but I have a dress fitting. Unless you'd like to come with me? You can see Wrenn and my mom."

"Will there be food after?" I ask, and my stomach grumbles.

"Yes, we're going out of town for lunch, though. My mom wants to try a new place we've never been. Maybe eat a granola bar now to tide you over?"

"Sounds good." I nod and look in the cabinets. There are several boxes of granola and protein bars. I grab a peanut butter chocolate chip one and follow Alana to the car.

Her car is much nicer than mine. I'm due for an upgrade, especially with how much I've been driving the last few years, but I'm putting it off. The last thing I want is to accidentally buy a dud car and end up in the shop every few weeks. Alana's leather seats and sleek BMW is making me reconsider.

"I think I found the perfect dress, but I haven't seen it in my size yet. So that's what I'm trying on today. If it fits then it'll just need some small alterations closer to the wedding," Alana explains.

"That's awesome! Have you picked out the wedding colors yet?" Last I heard, she was between two different palettes and couldn't finalize the details until she chose.

"Yes, I'm going with silver and navy. Very sleek and sophisticated—like Will and I," she says proudly.

"I love it."

"While we're here, you can pick your maid of honor dress. I have a few different choices so everyone can pick one they feel most comfortable in, and the color will be matching."

"That's smart." And silently, I'm relieved. It's not a secret that I'm fat; it's something I own. But I'm worried about the fact that most of Alana's bridesmaids are on the slimmer side. I didn't know if we'd all be forced to wear the same dress that was bound to be unflattering on someone. I should've realized Alana is more thoughtful than that.

"Wrenn said she's here, but she's waiting in her car. Our mothers still aren't getting along." Alana sighs.

"Well, it wouldn't be a wedding without a little family drama," I joke to ease the tension.

Alana's too busy frowning and checking her phone. I catch Will's name out of the corner of my eye, but I don't look at the message. If she wants to talk about it, she will.

Alana's sister is only a few years younger than us with the same dark brown hair as hers. While Alana is more reserved in the way she dresses and expresses herself, Wrenn is more outgoing. She's covered in piercings, tattoos, and ripped clothes. I think that's why their mom has a hard time accepting Wrenn. Personally, I love the way she expresses herself, but I'm also not her mother. Her mother is a more uptight version of Alana. I've had the pleasure of meeting her several times over the years, and she always smiles like someone made her wear panties that were three sizes too tight.

"Hello dear," her mother greets us at the door of the shop. She gives Alana a swift hug and smiles at me. The same smile as usual.

"Hey mom." Wrenn waves and her mother's face changes.

"Really? Ripped jeans? Do you not have enough money for pants without holes in them?" Her mother sighs, and Wrenn rolls her eyes as she follows her into the shop.

Alana whispers something to Wrenn, and she disappears into the store. Someone comes over to help us, and Alana and her mom explain what they're looking for. I start looking at the dresses on the racks, wondering what dresses might be mine. A lot of them are in smaller sizes, which is typical. It's rare to see anything over a large in stores, let alone a 4 or 5 XL.

Wrenn reappears holding a silk red dress with a slit up the side, and while Alana loves it, her mother immediately tells her to put it back. She returns with a similar dress five minutes later, only this time, there's no slit up the side. I can tell her mother is looking for a reason to trash it, so I jump in.

"I like it. Seems like it could be a cool bridesmaid's option." I smile. Wrenn beams at me and their mother nods.

Eventually they bring over Alana's dress and show her to the fitting rooms. I take a seat on the couch across from her mom, and Wrenn plops down next to me.

"I know you're just being nice because my mom sucks," Wrenn whispers.

"I'm always nice," I tease.

"What do you guys think?" Alana steps out, and my jaw drops.

Even in just normal makeup and a basic ponytail, Alana looks amazing in this dress. It's got lace sleeves, creating a sheath overlay of the ivory dress. It fits Alana's curves and shows off her chest. There's a long train that flows behind her like a royal.

"This is *the* dress right?" I ask.

"I think so, what do you guys think?" Alana chews on her bottom lip nervously and pulls at the fabric by her waist.

"You look beautiful, dear. I think it's perfect." Her mom is even tearing up a little.

"You look really good, Sis. I think you should get it," Wrenn agrees.

"It's like this dress was made for you," I add.

"Okay. I think I might do it in white instead of ivory. But I really like it." She smiles.

We all agree it looks perfect on her, and Alana seems to relax a bit. I've never known her to need anyone else's reassurance but her own. It seemed like she was really doubting her instincts on this one. Her mom helps her out of the dress while Wrenn and I wait. We're offered champagne, which I happily take a glass of.

"Next time I'm making Alana drive if there's going to be drinks," Wrenn mumbles to herself.

Alana and her mom come out of the dressing room and head to the front to pay. Wrenn and I decide to hang out front and give them a chance to settle everything in private. I can only imagine how much a dress like that might cost. Not that they'd have any trouble paying for it.

"Are you in town long?" Wrenn asks, looking up from her phone.

"Yeah, actually. I'm here until the end of September."

"Nice! You might be a good buffer between me and my mother."

"I'm sorry she gives you a hard time." I sigh. I didn't have any advice to offer, but it can't be easy.

"It is what it is." She shrugs.

Alana and her mom open the doors, and Wrenn pushes off the side of the building with her foot. I follow Alana to the car with the hope of food in the nearby future. That granola bar I had just isn't cutting it. Alana is quiet as we drive to the restaurant, and I wonder if it's the wedding or the dress or something else. But she seems to be contemplating something, so I keep quiet for now and make a mental note to check in soon. If she doesn't come clean about what's wrong, I'll eventually drag it out of her. Because that's what best friends do.

THREE

Norah

I've seen evidence of Gemma living in the house with me, but we've been on such opposite schedules that I haven't actually met her yet. It's sort of eerie living with someone I don't know, but I remind myself college was the same at first. There's another towel in the bathroom, extra shoes by the door and food I didn't cook in the fridge. Small things. If I didn't know better, it would make me think I'm going nuts. Alana mentioned Gemma works at Lovers General Hospital as a nurse, so it makes sense that I haven't seen her much. I think she's been doing the morning shifts, and I've been getting home when she's already sleeping. Today, I've made it a point to not make any plans after work so I can introduce myself to her. Hopefully she doesn't go to bed the moment she gets home. It would be nice to put a face to my new roommate.

"You're not going to get your sandwich before you leave? It's Wednesday. You always have your sandwich from the deli on Wednesdays." Sutton quirks an eyebrow when I tell her I want to head straight home.

"I have leftovers at home that I don't want to go to waste," I lie smoothly.

"Ah, well enjoy!" Sutton smiles and I slip out the front door.

I hate lying to Sutton, but I'm not ready to talk to anyone about what's going on. I've cut out cold cuts the last few weeks too, but I managed to at least walk toward the deli and take the long way to the parking lot. Today, I didn't have the time, and I didn't think Sutton would notice. As I walk the quick way to my car, I think about telling her. But then I shake my head, thinking better of it. It's not like she'd freak out or anything, but I want to do this alone—at least until it's okay to tell people.

Three months ago, I walked into the old fertility clinic just outside town and asked them to explain the process of IVF. When Finn was still alive, we had been starting the process ourselves. After years of trying to get pregnant with no success, we asked for help. We were all ready. There were so many steps involved on my end—and even on Finn's end. We got all the way to the embryo transfer, but that was the day of Finn's accident, so I obviously didn't go through with it. Everything was put on hold, the embryos were kept on ice, and I always thought we'd try again when Finn recovered. But surgery after surgery only proved that we'd never have that chance.

I've kept the embryos frozen, just in case. I never thought I'd actually use them, but I didn't have the heart to just toss them away. I mean, I had wanted to be a mom with Finn, not on my own. I let myself grieve in my own time, and while I'm still grieving, I know this is something I want. Finn would want us to have kids. So, I restarted the process and used our embryos. On Monday, I have an appointment to see if it worked—which is why I've cut out cold cuts, just to be on the safe side. I'm going to take every precaution necessary.

I skipped my last two appointments, afraid to go in and have them tell me it didn't work. I'm still terrified, but I need to know. I can't risk not knowing any longer and accidentally putting the baby in danger because I'm scared. I figure if it didn't work, then maybe it's not in the cards for me. I can always look into fostering or adopting at another point.

By the time I get home, I notice Gemma's car in the driveway and hope she's still awake. I walk inside, slip off my flats, and peek my head in each room as I walk toward the kitchen.

"Hi." I smile when I see Gemma's back turned to me. Dressed in a T-shirt and leggings, she's got both fridge doors open and is balancing two containers in one hand. Spinning around, she gasps, drops the food and screams when she sees me.

"Holy shit. I'm so sorry!" She gasps. Gemma pulls out an AirPod from one ear, and I wince.

"I'm sorry. I said hi!" I step forward to help her clean up. The containers are thankfully shut tight, so nothing spilled out.

"No, it's my fault. I didn't know what time you'd be home, so I didn't want to blast music, but I should've only had one in or something." She laughs.

"No worries."

Gemma picks up the containers and starts making a plate of the leftovers she must've made at another time. It looks like chicken with some kind of pasta. After looking at the food, I look at Gemma. What happens next nearly knocks me off my feet.

Her melted chocolate-brown eyes meet mine, and I freeze. Her lips are painted a soft pink, her dark curls frame her face, and her cheeks have a slight pink blush. She is freaking gorgeous. Gemma's wearing a T-shirt that says *Harvard* on it, and her curves are filling it out. I step back, surprised at how much this woman has me startled. I've always appreciated other women, but I've never been *into* other women.

"Do you want some?" Gemma asks, and I realize she thinks I'm staring at her food.

"No, that's okay. I was just going to make a peanut butter and jelly for dinner. It's been a long day." I smile and head to the fridge for my ingredients.

"Alana said you work at the bookstore, right?"

"Yup. I'm technically a manager now. But it's a fancy title with not too many benefits." I blush. *Why am I suddenly heating up?*

"I love reading. I'll have to stop in one day." She smiles. Her teeth are perfectly white and straight, almost as perfect as that guy at work the other day.

"That'd be cool." I nod.

"So, do you want to, like, split any chores or groceries or anything? I don't wanna mooch off you, and I can help around the house."

"Oh, I didn't even think of that," I admit. "Maybe you can do the dishes? I sort of hate doing them."

"Done! No biggie for me."

"As for groceries, I'm happy to go shopping. I think Alana said you work mornings, but I can't imagine you have an easy schedule."

"I do twelve-hour shifts, three days on and three days off. So yeah, I can contribute money and maybe make a list? If you don't mind doing the shopping."

"That's okay with me," I agree.

"Maybe we should exchange numbers, just in case one of us needs something, or God forbid the house is on fire?" Gemma chuckles nervously.

"Yeah, of course." I pull out my phone as Gemma recites her number. I shoot her a quick text, and a second later, her phone dings.

"I was going to watch a movie in the living room if that's cool?"

"Yes, please. This is your place as much as mine so do whatever. I've been told I'm fairly easy to live with."

"Same here. No stress, and I sleep a ton so I'm quiet too," she adds with a laugh.

"Then we'll get along great. I'm going to eat this in bed, but I'll see you around." I smile, grabbing my sandwich and retreating to the bedroom.

My room is dark, so I flip on the lamp, put my sandwich on the nightstand, and decide to take a quick shower first. I hate getting into the bed with outside clothes on. Especially ones I wore all day at work. I toss them in the laundry, turn on the hot water, and melt my muscles away.

I use the lavender body soap to relax myself and the pomegranate pumice to scrub away the dead skin. I shampoo and condition my naturally red hair and shave my legs smooth. I'm beginning to relax when Gemma pops into my head. I start to wonder why she had such an impression on me. It isn't like I'm new to meeting people; I see tons of people every day. It's tourist time in the summer, and To Be Loved is a hot spot. But when I met Gemma, it felt *different* and yet *familiar* all at once. I can't put my finger on it.

I'm not worried about being roommates with her. If she's someone Alana trusts, then so do I. But there was something off about our first encounter. I'd have to see how it feels being around her again tomorrow.

Once the bathroom is steaming up like a sauna, I decide I'm clean enough. Relaxed, I step out of the water and dry my body off with a fluffy towel. I wipe off the mirror that's covered in condensation and brush my hair. As the mirror clears, I glance at my body. I know it's silly to think I'd be able to tell if I was pregnant already. It's not like I suddenly have a baby bump and don't know it. But still, I glance at my side profile and touch my firm but thin stomach. I place a hand over it and close my eyes, just for a second, to wonder.

"It'll happen when it's supposed to," Finn's voice fills my ears.

My eyes shoot open, and tears brim on the surface. It isn't the first time I've heard him talk to me. I know it's just my imagination, but sometimes I wonder if he's really with me. I like to think he's around somewhere watching over me. But I don't know.

I wrap my towel around me and head into the bedroom. I get dressed in my cozy cotton T-shirt that belonged to Finn and a pair of shorts. I slide into bed and eat my sandwich while scrolling on my phone. Mindless videos of people cleaning carpets and people dancing. I was trying to distract myself, but there's only one way to do that.

I grab my Kindle from the charger, my fluffy white blanket, and head to the spare room. It's become a bit of a nightly ritual—I retreat into the spare room, get comfortable on the lounge chair, and read before bed. The spare room is covered in bookshelves; Alana said her mother used to escape here to read when she was a kid. The bookshelves mainly have romances and fiction books, which happen to be my favorite genres. Sometimes I pick a book from the shelf, but sometimes I grab one at work and sometimes I read on my Kindle.

The lounge chair I'm sitting on is right next to the window that overlooks the Lovers Lighthouse. At this time of night, you can see the sun setting perfectly behind it. Sometimes there are boats sailing by or people that look as tiny as ants. It's incredibly relaxing to watch such a view. The other side of the room had a built in bookshelf with a built in couch. It's equally as comfortable, but it doesn't have this view. Many nights, I've fallen asleep in here too. Especially lately.

It's peaceful no matter what time of day it is. I can sip tea, read a book, or just look out the window for hours. It's my way of being able to escape lately. When I'm in this room, it's like all my problems are left outside. Sure, they'll be there when I get back. But for now, for a few hours, they aren't my problem anymore. I could escape to a small town with a hero who just has to have the heroine, or I could read an emotional journey that makes me cry.

The character's problems are never as bad as mine, and they remind me mine will eventually pass too.

FOUR

Gemma

The credits of *Twilight* play, and I turn off the TV. I'm not ashamed to admit it's a comfort movie. Somewhere in the past, little Gemma was squealing at the first time Edward and Bella kissed. I was obsessed with the books and movies as a kid. The obsession turned into a normal amount of like, and the movies became my guilty pleasure. Something about rewatching them as an adult gives me some comfort.

I bring my plate to the kitchen and wash the dishes, just like I promised Norah I would. Drying my hands, I head to my room to find my Kindle. On the way there, I notice Norah sitting in the spare room that looks more like a library. She looks cozy under a fluffy blanket by the window. She's too busy reading on the device to notice me. I find my Kindle in my room and think about joining Norah. I don't want to step on any toes, but it looks so cozy in there. Maybe she wouldn't mind it if I sat in there with her. I grab a blanket off my bed and head back to the room.

"Hey, do you, umm, mind if I'm in here too? Just to read." I hold up my Kindle as if to show proof I won't be a bother. Norah looks up from her book and smiles.

"Yeah, of course." She sits up a little straighter and yawns.

I sit on the adjacent couch, my back to the wall, and I drape the blanket over my legs. I turn on my Kindle and click on the book I'm reading. It's a queer small town romance, so it's not like I left off on a suspenseful part of the book. The couple finally got together, so they're about to go on their first official date. I'm trying to focus on the book, but Norah is low key distracting me with her facial expressions. She's furrowing her brows, biting her bottom lip, and rolling her eyes as she reads. She probably has no idea she's doing it, but since she's in my peripheral vision, it's sort of distracting.

Norah wasn't at all what I was expecting when Alana talked about her. I'm not entirely sure what I was expecting. Norah is drop dead gorgeous. Her long red hair reminds me of the Little Mermaid's. She has these light green eyes and pale skin with just a few freckles across her nose. She's quite thin but surprisingly almost as tall as my five foot eleven. I know she's our age, but she looks too young to have already been married. Though, I guess Alana is our age and getting married too. It's just weird to think about anyone our age being married.

I'm so far off from that stage in my life. I can't remember the last time I was in a serious and committed relationship. It isn't that I'm against it, but it doesn't make sense for me to start something when I know I'm going to be leaving soon. The most I ever stayed in one place was six months, and that was no time to start something new. Besides, I never know where I might end up next, and I hate the idea of a long distance relationship. I guess I'll eventually choose one place to stay if it's for the right woman.

Norah yawns again and reminds me I should be reading. I want to finish this book before bed, and I won't if I don't get focused. So I turn my head and keep reading. I have work early in the morning, and although I only need a few hours of sleep, I don't want to be up all night. Around nine p.m., I finish the book and collect my things.

"Headed to bed?" Norah asks.

"Yeah, I have to be there at five," I explain.

"Oof. Well, goodnight."

"Goodnight." I smile.

Heading to bed, I have a good feeling about staying here this summer. Living with Norah is like hitting the roommate lottery.

It's my fourth, maybe fifth shift at Lovers General Hospital, and I've only gotten lost twice. Once was on my first day when I got turned around on my way to radiology, and the second was today, when I forgot where the break room is. Thankfully, one of my coworkers took pity on me and walked me there. I'm still not sure of names, but the nursing supervisor I report to is kind. She checks in with me every day to make sure I have what I need for the day and reminds me I can stop by her office if I need anything. I work in the emergency department, so it's rare I'm going to need any help from her with patients. But it's nice to know she's one of the supervisors who cares about her employees. I've worked in plenty of places where the staff was just as rude as some patients.

Once I put my lunch away in the break room and tighten my hair into a ponytail, I head to the ER. It's morning in a small town, so thankfully, it's not too crowded. There's a sick kid in bed one and two drunk adults in bed five. I assume they're keeping them apart on purpose. I grab an iPad and head to bed one to check on the patient. Only intake is done, so I need to do an initial evaluation before the doctor stops by. I'll get vitals and a rundown of the symptoms she's having.

"Hi, I'm nurse Gemma. What seems to be going on today?" I look at both mom and the girl. She's only six, so although she can talk for herself, her mother is probably going to speak for her.

"This is Carolyn, she woke up last night at three a.m. with a fever of 104.5 and hasn't been able to drink or eat anything," her mother explains.

"Got it. Can I take a look?" I look at Carolyn, who nods, and I take her temperature first: 101.3. Not great considering they gave her Tylenol not too long ago.

I take a quick peek down her throat, and it's completely raw and red. It looks like strep with the white on her tonsils, but I don't say that out loud. We'd need a test and the doctor's confirmation on that. I punch in the details on the iPad and order a strep test with flu and others just to be careful.

"Okay, I ordered some tests so I'll run those quickly with a throat swab and then the doctor will be by with results." I smile. Carolyn winces in anticipation of the test.

I grab gloves and the tests from behind the nurses' station and swab her throat. She holds her mother's hand tightly and gags when I rub the cotton swab down her throat. I've had my fair share of swabs, so I know it isn't fun.

"Why don't I see if we can grab you some ice from the nurse's station?"

Carolyn nods happily.

"Thank you," her mother adds.

I run the test over to the station for collection and then type in some quick notes. Then, I check on bed five and try to compose my face when the smell of urine hits me.

"Hi, gentlemen. How are we today?" Only one of them is in the bed but they both look drunk off their asses to me. The older one in the bed has a clear urine stain on the front of his dark jeans.

"Well, I told him I'm fine! But noooo, all because I tripped, he *insisted* that we come here." The older man is slurring his words and talking quite loudly.

"Did you hit your head when you fell?" I ask. God, the smell is killing me, but I need to keep composure. Another two minutes and I can make an excuse to get some fresh air.

"No." He shakes his head.

"His arm is bleeding," the second guy adds. He points to the right side and holds up the older man's bleeding forearm.

"Can I have a name for you? It seems like there isn't one in the system." I frown.

"Oh, surely. I'm Bob and this is John." The older man laughs.

"And last name?"

"Smith." They both say bursting out in laughter.

"Alright." I've dealt with my fair share of drunk idiots. And drunk people who didn't have health insurance who give fake names.

"I'll be right back to clean that up. Do you need a change of clothes or a gown to wear in the meantime?" I ask.

"What? Why?" Bob looks at me like I'm the crazy one.

"Because you pissed yourself man! I told you I smelled piss!" John starts cracking up as Bob realizes his mistake.

"Bring me your fanciest gown! And a scotch on the rocks." Bob winks.

I just nod and check to see if we have any spare scrubs. In some of the hospitals I've been in, we have spare sets in case anyone unhoused comes in and needs a set. I find a set in his size and bring them over, giving him a moment to change. Then I toss his clothes in a laundry bag and place it on the hook behind him. I put on fresh gloves and set up a tray to clean up his wound. It's superficial but dirty with what looks like mud and gravel. I irrigate it and put on antibiotic cream to prevent infection. I set up an IV bag to help with his dehydration and head back to the nurse's station.

"Everything alright?" My coworker with dark long hair and tattooed arms asks.

"Peachy. How was your break?" I smile.

"Eh, I napped for most of it in my car and then chugged a protein shake. I'm ready for this day to be over." She shrugs.

"Have you worked here long?" I take a seat next to her behind the nurses' station.

"Since I graduated college, so about six or seven years now."

She nods. I discreetly glance at her name tag hanging out of the pocket of her scrubs: Nurse Gloria.

"Are you a local?"

"No, I was born in Vermont, but I went to college in Maine. I did my rotations here and then just decided to stay. It's pretty relaxed as far as ERs go. I have friends who moved to New York after college, and all I hear are horror stories. I don't think I could handle that," she explains.

"I've worked in some big ERs, and it's not for the lighthearted," I agree.

Lovers is definitely more tame than some of the other places I've worked. I think there are only fifty nurses total in the whole hospital which includes all the specialties and the labor unit. When I worked in New York, there were at least fifty nurses in the ER alone. I didn't mind it, but I have to admit, working somewhere so relaxed has its benefits.

Around thirty minutes later, the doctor comes down to check out Carolyn's results, and I was right, it's strep. She gives a prescription for a round of penicillin and instructs the mom to keep her home from school for forty-eight hours or until she's been fever free for at least twenty-four. Bob and John eventually head home and in comes the next round of patients. There are two moms in labor who get sent almost immediately to labor and delivery, a teenager who ends up having mono, and a couple who just got back from their honeymoon who both have UTI's. That was a fun one to explain. When I told them they should refrain from sexual intercourse for the next two weeks, they both frowned like I handed them a death sentence.

I wish someone would be upset they couldn't have sex with me. Then at least I'd be having sex. I know I'm not dating, but it's been too long since I've been laid. My vibrator is worn out, and I'm tired of replacing the batteries.

FIVE

Norah

"Miss Perry?" the nurse calls rather loudly, and I wince.

"Here." I smile and grab my purse, following her into the back room of the offices.

"Okay, you'll strip from the bottom down and place this over your legs. The doctor will be in shortly for an ultrasound," he explains. I nod and take the paper sheet from him.

He leaves the room, and I slide out of my leggings and tuck my panties in the pocket of my jeans. It's not like I'm trying to hide my panties. In a moment the doctor will be seeing, well, *everything*. But I don't want to lose them either. I sit on the exam table and drape the sheet over my legs. At least I remembered to shave today. Not that my doctor would care about that either. I'm just so nervous. I've already given a whole array of answers on a very personal medical form and a cup of my urine. They are about to confirm that the four pregnancy tests I took at home were accurate.

There's a light knock on the door, and I manage to say, "Come in."

"Hello, Norah. I'm Dr. Greenwald. It's nice to meet you." She smiles and shakes my hand.

She looks maybe a decade older than I am, with a chopped blonde bob and red lipstick. She's wearing a tight pencil skirt and a blouse under her doctor's coat. She looks over her clipboard of notes from me and then sits down on the small rolling stool across from me.

"Okay, so it looks like you've tried IVF at the local office. And I see here you've gotten a positive result on at home pregnancy tests?"

"Yes. I took four of them," I add.

"Okay, we don't have your urine results back yet. So let's take a look with the sonogram machine." She puts down the clipboard and turns on the oversized machine next to me.

I pull up my shirt and wait as she puts on fresh gloves, then puts the cool gel on my stomach. I watch the machine carefully, hoping for some sign of *something*. I don't really know what I'm supposed to be looking for, but I don't take my eyes off the screen. She moves the wand across my stomach and is quiet as she looks. I could never be a doctor; my face would give everything away too easily.

"It looks like I can't get a good read through your stomach, which is normal to start. So I'm going to have to look vaginally, is that okay?" I nod and she wipes the goo off my stomach, covers me up, and then relocates between my legs.

It feels like a bit of pressure but I try not to tense up as she moves the wand around. All of a sudden there's a dull thudding sound coming from the machine and a pulsing light in the blur of black and white.

"There is the fetus." She points to the screen. "This is the heartbeat, which is nice and strong like we want it."

My own heart stops. The IVF worked. There's a baby. My baby.

My and Finn's baby.

"You look to be about six weeks along. Which is right according to your implantation date. I'm going to do a few measurements, but you're definitely pregnant." She smiles. "This is a pregnancy you'd like to continue, correct?"

"Yes! Definitely!" I all but yell at her.

"I'll print out some photos for you to take home. I'll give you a folder full of helpful things to keep you healthy during pregnancy. No hot tubs, alcohol, or drugs, and I need to see you back here in four weeks."

"Okay." I nod. The screen is frozen on the image of the baby blob, even though she's since removed the wand. My baby. My little blob that I'm growing in my own uterus. I could cry.

"I'll let you get dressed, and then you can come next door to my office."

She leaves and I get dressed, but everything is in slow motion. I'm *pregnant*. I can't imagine a time when I didn't want to be a mom. When everyone else was playing on the playground, I was playing with dolls and babysitting as much as I could. I loved children. I always dreamed of having a big family and lots of children. Finn and I wanted at least four. This last year made me think it was out of the cards for myself. But now I know it isn't. I'm going to be a *mom*.

I grab my purse before heading next door to Dr. Greenwald's office. She hands me a multitude of paperwork, explains how the appointments work, and tells me I should try not to miss any moving forward. She gives me a little goody bag with prenatal vitamins samples, a baby hat, and a handful of coupons for baby stuff. By the time I'm walking out of her office, I'm feeling a little overwhelmed.

As I drive back to the house, I think about how I wish I had someone to tell. Finn would obviously be my first call, and in a perfect world he would've been there with me today. I know I'm not ready to tell my friends or coworkers yet. But it isn't like I have any family I can tell. My parents died when I was in college, and I'm an only child. I'm close with Finn's mother, but I can't imagine calling her up to tell her the news. Especially this early. It feels like bad luck or something. God forbid something were to happen, then we'd both have another loss to mourn. I don't think I could do that to her.

But I know I need to tell someone. So when I pull in the driveway, I immediately turn around and drive to the other side of town. I haven't been here in the last few weeks. I've been trying to limit how often I come. Finn wouldn't want me living at the cemetery. There are unfamiliar flowers on his grave, which must mean his mother was here recently. They're wilting, so I replace them with some chrysanthemums I got on the way in.

"Hi, babe." I sit down on the grass in front of his grave. "I went to the doctor today. Turns out the IVF worked. We're going to have a baby!" I say aloud, and the tears come pouring down my face. They're like a waterfall I can't stop.

"I'm so happy, but God, I wish you were here. The baby is just a little blob, but I know she or he is going to be so beautiful." I pull out the sonogram from my pocket and face it toward the gravestone.

"This is our little miracle," I say in between sobs.

It's quiet here because it's during the day. Everyone else is usually at work. You can hear the water not too far from here. The waves crashing and the wind blowing in the distance. It's calming. His mother and I picked out this spot. Finn and I had will's, but we never picked out a plot or planned funeral arrangements. We both thought we'd have more time.

"I'll draft up a new will, make sure that if something happens to me that our baby will be taken care of. I promise," I say aloud. I hate to think about something like that, but it isn't like I can ignore the elephant in the room. You never knew when your time might be up.

I just need some time to think about who might get the baby. Finn and I had passing conversations about it, but nothing was ever finalized when he was still alive. I make a mental note to call the lawyer later. I want to get this process started as soon as possible.

I look over the letters on his stone.

Finn Perry, beloved son & husband.

It pains me to know he never got to be a father. He loved and wanted kids as much as me. I hate that I'm going through this alone, but I hate even more that I don't get to experience this with him. He was always making those terrible dad jokes and was so excited just at the idea of us being pregnant. I close my eyes and I can see him again. He's holding me close, and I swear for a second, I can feel his arms around me.

"I'll be back. And I'll bring the baby, too. They'll know their dad. I promise." I stand up, touch a hand to the stone, and then head down the path.

My parents were buried just several rows over. Of course this was what they had wanted. I was a later in life baby, and they had a will that planned every detail of their death and funeral. Buried in the same plot, my father first and then six months later, my mother. I sit on the grass next to their stone and replace the flowers I brought last time.

I tell them about the baby, and I wonder how they would've been as grandparents. They were amazing parents, always there for me and always supporting me. I can only imagine they'd be even better grandparents. This baby would be incredibly loved. It *will* be incredibly loved.

My parents lived their entire lives in Lovers. Got married right out of high school and settled in town. They traveled the world in their twenties and ran a successful law firm in town. By the time I was born they were closer to retirement and made the rest of their lives about me. I never got to ask if they had wanted kids all along, because it didn't matter. I was there and they never made me feel bad about being around.

On the way out of the cemetery, I toss the old flowers away. There's a spot to toss them so they can turn them into mulch. Much better than just disposing of them.

When I get to my car, I turn it on because it's hotter than I realize in the sun. I blast the AC, but I don't move. I do some deep breaths and try to relax myself. I pull out the ultrasound and stare at it again. It's nothing more than an oddly shaped blob. But for some reason, this blob is bringing me to tears. I grab some napkins from McDonalds from my glove compartment and wipe my face off. Good thing I didn't bother putting on makeup this morning. I knew I might be somewhat of a mess. Pregnant or not.

I wish I had someone to share this news with. But in time, I will. My friends, although they'll be surprised, will be happy for me. They know how long I've wanted this. They'll be my biggest supporters. I just want to make sure I have happy news to tell them. For too long now, my friends have looked at me with sad puppy dog eyes. I know they mean well, but I'm tired of being treated with kid gloves. Maybe this will finally convince them that I'm doing okay.

I pull into the driveway, and Gemma isn't home yet. So I sneak into my room and hide all the baby stuff in my sock drawer. I don't think she will come in my room for anything, but I'm still not ready to have it all out on display. If she finds out and tells Alana, it might be a bit too much for her, especially before the wedding. I know firsthand how stressful weddings can be, so I don't want her to have to worry about a pregnant bridesmaid.

SIX

Gemma

I'm at Alana's house right after work—two iced coffees in hand. She didn't ask for one, but I have a feeling it's going to be a long night. Plus, I know her usual order. Alana answers the door with her dark black hair piled on her head in a messy bun with strands falling out all over the place. She's barefaced and even wearing her glasses instead of contacts. Shit, she might be in worse shape than I thought.

"I brought coffee, and I'm all yours. Tomorrow is my day off." I smile.

"Thank goodness. I needed this." She accepts the iced coffee from me, takes a long sip, and smiles. "You remembered how I like it."

"Of course." I nod. I didn't get to be maid of honor by slacking.

"Come in, come in." She waves me in, and I slide off my sneakers and follow her to the dining room.

"So, what's going on?" All she had said on the phone was she needed maid of honor help.

"Okay, so. Will is finalizing the invitations to go out this week. I'm going to triple check when he gets back from his work thing tomorrow night. But I need to finalize the seating chart."

"How can you make a seating chart if the invitations aren't back yet?" I ask, tilting my head at her. Across the table is a foam board with lots of circles and colored post-its.

"We sent everyone a digital invitation. They RSVP'd through there. The physical invitations are more of a keepsake than anything else. We're just sending them to all the people who replied yes," she explains.

"Makes sense." I nod. Alana takes a seat at the head of the table, so I sit next to her.

"I just need to finalize the headcount, send all the names for place cards to the woman making the cards, and then order the last few items."

"Okay, so tell me where I can help, and you relax."

"Can you do the seating chart? You know who mostly everyone is. Will's side of the family is done; it's just my side, so you know who can be near each other."

"Sure." I nod.

I place my iced coffee on a coaster she has handy in the middle of the table, and then I get started. I look at all the labeled people and begin arranging them as best as I can. It's sort of like Tetris. Everyone needs a seat, there's only so many seats at a table, and you can't split up certain families. It doesn't help that Alana's family is huge, and she's quite social, so she has a lot of friends. But I manage to piece my way through it.

Alana pulls out her laptop and begins typing away. She's scrunching her eyebrows together and sighing every so often. I can only imagine how stressful planning a wedding must be. I've been to my fair share of them, and they seem like a lot more effort than they're worth. Not that I'd dare say that to Alana. But, I just can't see myself going through a big wedding like this just for one day. I'd be much happier taking a woman down to city hall and marrying her there. After all, what is marriage anyway? A piece of paper saying all the stuff I'd be proving to someone every single day? I don't need to put on a big show for anyone.

"Do you want dinner? I'm going to order some pizza from the new place in town." Alana looks up from her computer.

"Sure. I'll have whatever you're having."

"Got it." She grabs her phone and heads into the kitchen. She comes back with a glass of water, and I realize she's already done with her iced coffee.

"I think I'm done with this," I say as I plop the final name back on the chart. I look it over again, counting to make sure each table only has eight chairs, and everyone is accounted for.

"Shit, you made it look easy. I was literally staring at this thing for hours and could not figure it out." She sighs. Snapping a photo of it first, she then moves it onto the cabinet she has behind the table.

"Have you been making time for self-care?"

"Do you mean masturbating?" Alana glances at me. Her words don't surprise me. You can't be roommates with someone for years and pretend you both don't masturbate.

"Well that's certainly one way. But no, I mean like getting a massage, relaxing and not thinking about wedding preparations? You seem super stressed," I point out.

"I mean…I am. But it's just because the wedding is soon. We have like, six weeks? There's so much to do and it's not like I hired a wedding planner." She sighs.

"But it's a lot for just one person. Why isn't Will helping out more?"

"Not this. I know he isn't your favorite—"

"No, this isn't about him. I promise. It's just, he should be helping and supporting you through this. I don't mind stepping in as long as he's doing his part too."

"He is! It's just he works so much and so hard, so it's sometimes easier for me to do things."

"I just don't want you to burn yourself out planning a perfect wedding."

"I won't. I'll be fine!"

Before she can insist anymore, the pizza delivery is here. She disappears while I make room on the table to eat. She drops off a small pizza box in front of me and another one in front of her. I open the steaming box to see a chicken parmesan hero—one of my absolute favorites. In college during exams, we'd have them delivered all the time and live off them. Our friends would complain, but hey, it's full of protein...and tomato sauce is sort of like a vegetable.

"I need ranch. Do you want some?" Alana asks, but I shake my head.

"So, when's the last time you got laid?" Alana asks bluntly, and I almost choke on my food.

"Excuse me?"

"Oh, you heard me. I'm guessing it's been awhile." She eyes me.

"Fine, yes. I've been busy with work and it's hard to find someone when I travel so much."

"Well, you should get on that. There will be a ton of queer women at my wedding. And in this town for that sake."

"Really?" I ask, surprised.

"Oh, yes. This town is like exceptionally queer for some reason. There just happen to be a lot of them." She shrugs.

"I guess I'll have to make sure I look extra good on your wedding day then."

"You better. I need absolute babes up there next to me." She smiles. "Speaking of my hot friends, how are you getting along with Norah?"

"Oh, she's cool," I say nonchalantly. But Alana must pick up on my nonchalance, so she raises an eyebrow.

"You said she was married right?" I tread lightly.

"Yeah, her husband, Finn, passed away like almost two years ago now." She sighs. "Why?"

"It's nothing, she just gives me this not so straight vibe." I shrug.

"Norah? Really?" I raise an eyebrow at her.

"Yeah, what?"

"Most of my friends are queer, but I've never heard that said about Norah. But maybe that's because she was with Finn since high school."

"It's not like she said anything; it's just a vibe."

"Huh, I didn't even consider her being with anyone else. She and Finn were like soulmates. When he died, it destroyed her. She's only just coming out of that now."

"She seems okay to me. Of course, I don't know her like you do."

"I'm glad you're staying with her. It'll be good for her to have you there. You've always been a great listener."

"Thanks." I smile.

I purposely leave out the part about how I'm attracted to Norah. It's only a harmless little crush, but I can't help it. Norah is beautiful, and we have a lot in common. Each night we spend hours in the spare room just reading books near each other. Sometimes we talk about the books we're reading or just ask how the other's day at work was. It was the best part of my day. I glance at the clock, I'll be missing it tonight, and part of me hates that.

I know it's stupid. I'm sure Norah doesn't even notice if I'm even there or not. But on the days when I sleep through it, I miss it in the morning. From the way Alana talks about Norah, I assumed to meet a grieving widow. Not that she couldn't be grieving in private, but she seems *okay*. I can't imagine the pain she went through of losing someone she loved. I'm sure it's something that she has daily reminders of. So it isn't like I'm going to ask and check in with her. But I hope someone in her life is.

"Do you need me to do anything else?" I ask while I clean up from dinner.

"Can you look over the headcount and see if it matches mine?" Alana smiles.

"Of course."

I dump the food containers in the kitchen, grab a glass of

water, and then return to the table. She's left a paper in front of me, so I look it over and then start my count. I count it twice and get the same number she has. Three hundred and fourteen guests. Jesus, she's planning for everyone she and Will know to come to this thing. It's suddenly daunting—the idea of walking down the aisle in front of so many people.

"I got the same count as you." I hand her back the papers.

"I was hoping I was overcounting." She sighs.

"Are three hundred and fourteen people really coming?"

"Yeah. My parents and Will's parents kept adding guests." She frowns. "My mother is convinced this is her only chance to plan a wedding."

"What about Wrenn?!" I gasp. It isn't like Alana is an only child.

"She's convinced she won't get married, even though I'm pretty sure Wrenn's always wanted to get married someday. But please don't tell her. I hate that my mom even said it to me."

"Wow. She really doesn't get along with your sister. I thought it was bad at the dress store, but damn."

"She just doesn't understand Wrenn. She does what she wants instead of what our mother thinks she should do."

"Yeah, I guess that's true. But it's not like you do *everything* your mother wants," I point out.

"Lately it's hard to see where my mother ends and where I begin." She sighs.

"I'm sorry. Is it because of the wedding?"

"Probably." She doesn't elaborate, but I'm not sure what to ask next.

"Anything else you need me to do?"

"Nope, thank you for coming over tonight. I know you had work today but I appreciate it." Alana smiles.

"What kind of maid of honor would I be if I didn't?"

"True. But go home and get some sleep."

"Thanks. I am ready to knock out," I say with a yawn.

I grab my stuff and head out to my car. It's still light out since it's only July, and the sun sets sometime after eight p.m. I put the address to home in the GPS. I'm not 100% sure where I'm going, and I don't want to get lost. I'm too tired for that. I silently wonder if Norah will still be reading when I get home. I try not to get my hopes up for a multitude of reasons. The last person I should be starting something with is Norah. I'm only here for a few months. I should be looking for a one-night stand. Not someone I want to see every day. Let alone, someone I have to see every day.

SEVEN

Norah

When I get home from lunch with Heather, I feel lighter. I've been holding on to the secret of the baby for four weeks now. It isn't a long time in the grand scheme of things, but it's long enough for me. I felt isolated long enough with my friends, and I don't want to keep hiding this. So, when Heather and I made lunch plans, I knew I needed to tell her. Plus, it is only right since I'll be naming her as the Godmother.

Finn and I weren't religious, but we weren't *not* religious. We went to church on Christmas with his family, and we had a church wedding. We didn't pray before our meals and go to church every Sunday, though. Finn had asked if we could do Godparents early into our marriage, quoting that it was something his mother would insist upon. I sort of liked the idea that our baby would be watched over and taken care of by someone if something were to happen to us. That's how we agreed on Heather. Despite all the years of friendship, we've always remained the closest of the group. She dropped everything to be there for me when my parents died. And she did the same when Finn died.

Finn and I had agreed she'd be the perfect Godmother. The

only problem is finding a Godfather. It isn't like I have a ton of male friends. And while Finn did, it's not like any of them are keeping in touch with me. Sure, for a while some of them did. But now we're just friends on Facebook who wish each other a happy birthday. I don't know any of them well enough to offer them my child.

I run into the house because I need to pee *again*. I thought peeing so much was for when I was actually showing. Not in the beginning when the baby is still as small as a rock. But I've peed several times today, and I still always need to go.

When I'm done, I head back outside to my car to grab my leftover desserts. Heather had insisted on treating me to all of them, and while I managed to eat some, I took the rest to go. So I find a spot for them in the fridge and then head to my room to change. These jeans are starting to get just a little too tight. I'd have to go the next size up in my closet.

I walk into the bathroom and glance in the mirror. I pull my shirt up and look to the side. There is a small but definable bump —to anyone who doesn't know better, which is everyone. I look like I had a big lunch, or like I'm a little bloated. I smiled, knowing that was just my baby growing. My boobs have grown two sizes, and I know it's only a matter of time before someone mentions that. It's not exactly like I can hide the fact that I went from an A cups to C in a matter of weeks. Despite the doctor telling me it's normal, it feels anything but.

I know what Finn would say; he'd be all over them. Which is another symptom of pregnancy no one warns you about: feeling extra horny. I've surprised the doctors by only having one bout of morning sickness so far. But everything feels like I want to get laid. Every nerve in my body is constantly on fire, and I think if I rubbed my thighs together, I could probably come from that. Or just touching my nipples. They're a tad bigger too, and fuck, even more sensitive than they used to be.

Just thinking about this makes me want to do something about it. Gemma isn't home, but I check the time. I still have at least two hours until she's home. I race back into my room and close the door just in case she gets home early. I scroll through my phone and pick up the latest Sara Cate book. Every time I read one of those, I'm dying to get off. I usually bookmark the scenes for times like this so I can find the spot I'm looking for.

I pull up the chapter and slide a hand up my chest. I tug lightly on my nipples and groan. God, that feels so good. Once they're both hardened, I slide my hand down my stomach and keep reading. It's a group scene with two women and a man, but it's like they're in bed with me. I don't know what it is about an FFM threesome that really gets me going. It's not something I've ever tried in real life. I keep reading, and I'm wetter with each page. I brush my thumb across my clit, and I actually gasp.

The women are going down on each other while the man is behind one of them, sliding in and out. I close my eyes to imagine that. Finn behind me and... Gemma in front of me. My eyes shoot open, but I don't move my hand. Gemma? I've never had a fantasy about her before. I mean, it's just a fantasy, who cares? I think she's beautiful, and it's not like I have any other contenders right now. I decide to close my eyes and go with it.

I'm moving my hand again across my clit in circles. My phone falls to the side, and I'm moving my hand faster through my folds and then back around my clit. I'm imagining the three of us in all sorts of positions that it feels so real. Her lips on mine, and Finn's hands on my body. Both of their lips on my neck. Fuck. Suddenly I'm seeing stars and screaming out a plethora of curses. Another thing no one talks about?

How amazing pregnancy orgasms can be.

I'm sitting in the spare room like I do every night. My Kindle, blanket, and a cup of tea are in my hand. I'm all cozy on the chair, glancing out the window when I hear Gemma clattering around in the kitchen. I think she's doing the dishes because I can hear the sink running, and there's a bit of clattering. Very lowly, I can also hear Gemma singing along to a song I don't recognize. She starts off humming and then it quickly turns into singing all the lyrics. She must have her headphones on again, because I can't hear any actual music playing.

I decide to wait until she's done to start reading. I don't need complete silence to read, but the singing is a bit distracting. I watch the sun set behind the lighthouse and five minutes later, Gemma's done, and the water stops—along with the singing. I start my book where I last left off. It's only when Gemma comes in with her stuff that I look up from my book. She gets settled on the couch across from me. We've made it somewhat of a habit to come in here every night. We both read quietly and then retreat to our own beds for the night. It's been quite nice actually.

"What are you reading?" she asks. Usually it's quiet once we both get settled, so I'm surprised.

"Oh, uh, the latest Sara Cate novel." I blush. Sara Cate has a bit of a reputation for writing "dirty" books.

"Which one? I *devoured* her last series. I didn't realize she wrote anything new," she says quickly, like she's excited from the news.

"*The Heartbreaker*? It's the third book in the Goode Brothers series."

"Third book?! I'm so behind! That's it. I'm downloading it right now." Gemma picks up her kindle to look for it.

"What were you reading?" I ask curiously.

"*Delilah Green Doesn't Care* by Ashley Herring Blake."

"I loved that book. The series was so cute." I smile.

"I have book two but now I'm torn because I wanna start the new Sara Cate book." She groans.

"Ah, the life of a reader." I laugh.

"Do you read fast? I have a lot of down time at work, so I'm always reading in-between patients. I don't know how fast I read, but I could definitely catch up on both series if I had work the next few days."

"I think I do? I kind of compete with my Kindle sometimes. It says the book will be over in like two hours, so I'll read to where I finish like fifteen minutes fast or something. It's silly."

"No! I do the same thing! Like I take the time as a challenge." We both laugh. It's nice to talk to someone who understands the reader side of me. Finn and I were compatible in so many ways, but reading was not one of them. He only liked to read the newspaper and perused the occasional article.

"Well, I'll let you read now. But when you're done, let me know what you think." I smile.

"Will do."

We both turn back to our books, and while I'm happy to get back to reading, I'm suddenly thirsting for more. I enjoy talking to Gemma. There's an ease about her. Maybe it's because she didn't know me and Finn, so she didn't know me before Finn's death. She only knows the me now. I think some people expect the old me to return one day. It isn't like I'm over here severely depressed, but I can't imagine turning back into that someone after the loss I've experienced. Gemma doesn't give me sad eyes or ask how I'm doing. She just talks to me like I'm a normal woman and now a widow—and I'm so grateful for that.

I sip my tea and mull over the taste. It isn't my favorite, but my stomach has been a little queasy since dinner, so I thought ginger tea might help. Maybe I should've just picked up some ginger candies on the way home. Thinking of candy makes me remember the desserts I have in the fridge. Ooh! One of those sounds so good right now. I had dinner earlier; lots of protein and greens. But now I want something sweet. This baby is giving me a bit of a sweet tooth lately. I get up, leaving my stuff behind, and then at the last second, I turn to face Gemma.

"Do you want dessert?"

"What are you offering?" she asks with a gleam in her eye.

"Everything." I wave for her to follow me and head for the kitchen.

Gemma's behind me as I grab the leftover containers and open each one. By the time I'm opening the fourth one, Gemma's eyeing me suspiciously. Oh, shit. I didn't realize how this must look to someone who doesn't know I'm pregnant. I look kind of crazy. I mean, who has this many leftover desserts for one person?

"My friend and I were celebrating something, and I ended up with all this extra dessert. So please help yourself," I explain shyly.

"This looks delicious. I was just surprised by the variety. It looks like you went to a bakery and couldn't decide." She laughs as I hand her a fork.

"Basically." I shrug.

"This is so good." She moans and it does something to my body I've never experienced before. All of a sudden, I'm thinking about my alone time earlier and how she popped up into my fantasy. I quickly shove a bite of cake into my mouth to distract myself.

She doesn't ask anything else and takes ownership of the apple crumble cake. While I dive into the molten lava cake, I realize it's surprisingly delicious even though it's cold. The chocolate lava is hardened like a chocolate goo, and it's even better than when it's hot. We're both having a foodgasm and giggling from the sugar high. I relax, letting my guard down a bit. Gemma smiles at me, and my stomach feels like Jell-O. I blame the sugar once again, even though I know it can't be.

EIGHT

Gemma

The doctor calls out, "Gemma?"

"Yes?" I turn to face them.

"I see you called for a pregnancy test, but it looks like that wasn't indicated. Can I ask why you did?" She taps on her clipboard and narrows her eyebrows at me.

"The patient mentioned a spotting period, swollen breasts, and has been throwing up lately. I know she came in for a flu test, but I thought it was best to rule out a pregnancy as well," I explain.

"Well, I'm glad you did. She is pregnant." Dr. Greenwald smiles as she hands me the chart. I've forgotten her name, so I'm grateful when I notice it's sewn onto her white coat.

"Oh." I don't want to say that's good, because who knows how the patient is going to take this kind of news.

"Do you want to come with me to tell her?"

"Sure." I nod and we head toward the room.

Once inside, I give the patient a comforting smile. "Okay, Mrs. Bortz. We have your results, and the flu test was negative, but you did test positive for pregnancy," Dr. Greenwald explains.

"Oh my goodness!" Mrs. Bortz gasps and her husband hugs her tightly.

"We've been trying for so long. This is amazing news." He smiles at us.

"I'm happy to provide a checklist of things to do next. I understand you're out of town, so once you get back home, I'd suggest you make an appointment with a local OBGYN. You'll want to get one as soon as possible."

"Yes, yes. Okay." Mrs. Bortz smiles. There are tears running down her cheeks.

Dr. Greenwald and I give them a moment alone and grab the paperwork to start discharge.

"Thank you for catching this. Not everyone does. We're lucky to have you here," Dr. Greenwald praises and disappears down the hall.

"Look at you go. Dr. Greenwald doesn't usually take a liking to someone so easily," Gloria muses.

"Really?"

"Yeah, she's a bit picky, but I guess you impressed her."

Gloria heads over to help bed six, so I take over watching the front desk. I guess it's pretty nice to impress a doctor. Especially when I was just doing my job. I also want to make sure every stone is unturned so the patient receives the best care.

"Hey, Gemma right?" one of the other nurses asks.

"Yeah." I nod. "What's up?"

"A bunch of us are getting dinner and drinks tonight at Teddy's. Would you like to come?"

"Sure." I smile. Only, I wish I knew this woman's name right now.

"I'm Elodie, by the way. We met your first day, but I'm sure that was overwhelming." She laughs.

"Yes, thank you. I'm so bad with names and learning everyone's at once is a lot."

"No worries. It's four or five of us—all nurses. I'll be sure to reintroduce you to everyone when you get there."

"Awesome. What time?"

"Six. We all get off at five."

"Okay, cool." I nod. That gives me enough time to go home to shower and change first.

"See you later." Elodie disappears down the hallway, and I get back to work.

Two children come in with their mom after they crashed their bikes into a tree. We set the mom up in between the two kids. One ended up with a broken leg, and the other has a fractured collarbone. I take them to radiology one at a time and promise to stay with them the whole time. The mom is on the younger side, and she looks worried, but I reassure her that this kind of thing happens all the time.

During the X-rays, I read on my Kindle in the hallway. I always keep it in my front pocket with my phone. It's easier this way. I hate just standing around with nothing to do, but I love reading, so I'll take it.

After the kids are released, the rest of my shift is mainly catching up on paperwork. Mostly the stuff I didn't get to look at this morning. By the time the night shift is coming in, I'm surprised at the time. Slow days are rare. I clock out alongside Gloria and Elodie, who says she hopes to see me later.

I grab my stuff from the locker, drive home, and am not surprised to find that Norah isn't home yet. I race through the shower, spending extra time on my hair and shaving my legs. Then I look for something to wear that isn't scrubs. I can't remember the last time I was in something other than scrubs, honestly. I find a pair of jeans and a black going out top. I switch out my sneakers for a pair of sandals and even throw on some makeup. When I stop to look in the mirror, I pause. I look good when I clean myself up.

Teddy's Bar & Grill is only five minutes away, and I don't want to be the first one there. So I clean up my bedroom a little while I wait for the time to pass. I need to do laundry when I get home. I'm on my last two pairs of clean scrubs. Checking my

Apple watch again, I realize it's time to go. I grab my car keys and head out. When I pull up to the place, it looks fairly busy for a random Wednesday night.

"Gemma! Over here!" Elodie calls when I walk in the front door.

She's sitting at a table with four other women I sort of recognize from work. I'm relieved it's a table and not a booth. Too many times have I tried shrinking myself into a booth only to feel suffocated while I eat. We all look different when we aren't in scrubs or carrying around a sample of urine with us. Elodie has beautiful long blonde hair that she keeps tied in a tight bun at work. She's wearing a dress that shows off her long tan legs.

"Gemma, this is everyone. Everyone this is Gemma." She smiles.

Everyone quickly introduces themselves to me again. Harriet has short auburn hair that she keeps in a bob. Cora has gorgeous thick curls that look soft enough to touch. Tilly has a cropped cut with the sides shaved, and Connie is sporting a sleek black ponytail. I'll clearly have to remember everyone by their hair color instead of their names.

"You just started in the ER, right?" Cora asks.

"Yeah, I mostly work mornings."

"I'm in the labor unit. Cora works in surgery, and Connie *and* Harriet are floaters." Tilly says.

"Have you been working here long?" I ask.

"We all started three years ago." Harriet smiles.

"Can I grab you a drink from the bar? I'm going to ask for some menus." Elodie asks.

"Sure, can you get me a glass of red wine?"

Elodie nods and heads toward the violet-haired bartender. Wait a second, was that Wrenn? I forgot she said she worked here.

"Excuse me, I just realized I know the bartender. I'll be right back." I excuse myself to go say hi.

Elodie quirks a brow when she sees that I've followed her. Wrenn doesn't notice me at first.

"What can I get you?" She doesn't look up from the pad of paper she's holding.

"Wrenn?" I smile.

"Oh, shit. Hey, Gemma!" She smiles.

"You guys know each other?" Elodie asks.

"She was college roommates with my sister," Wrenn explains.

"I'm actually here for the summer because she's getting married. I'm the maid of honor," I say proudly to Elodie.

"Oh, wow! That's awesome."

"Can I get you something to drink?" Wrenn asks.

"Just a red wine and some menus for the table, please," Elodie says.

"Of course. Amber will be your server, just flag her down when you know what you want." Wrenn hands Elodie the menus.

"I have to get back to work, but I'll see you around okay?" Wrenn smiles.

"Yes." I nod as she hands me the glass of red wine.

Elodie and I walk back to the table and rejoin the group. I explain how I know Wrenn and then the topic is on the wedding.

"I love weddings. Most of my friends got married right out of college. I'm the last lone wolf." Connie shrugs.

"Same here. Alana's one of the last to get married. Now me, who knows if I ever will," I say before sipping my wine.

"Marriage isn't for you?" Elodie guesses.

"I don't know. If the right person asked, I guess I'd accept, but I could live without it too."

"Makes sense. Hell of a lot cheaper than planning a wedding." Harriet laughs.

"Do you remember Dr. Emory's wedding? He spent almost a million on it and then was divorced a year later."

"Now that's just terrible."

We stop to look over the menus, everyone hungry from a

long day at work. I order a round of hot wings and some quesadillas. Our food is out fifteen minutes later, and it all looks delicious. I love bar food, it's rarely a disappointment. Everything is greasy and fried and tastes like heaven. As we dig in, Elodie goes on about the upcoming charity fundraiser.

"It's so much fun! We did it last year, but everyone from the hospital takes turns running a booth outside for the day."

"Like a carnival?" I guess.

"Yes! There's food and games and rides. It helps raise money for different charities, and the hospital usually matches whatever we raise," Harriet explains.

"That's awesome. I'd love to sign up if I still can."

"Yes, remind me next time you work, and I'll show you the sign up form." Elodie smiles.

I finish my glass of wine and switch to water. I'm driving home, and although it's close, I don't want to risk it. Everyone else is two or three drinks deep—except Harriet. Maybe she's some sort of designated driver tonight. Either way, everyone is a good level of buzzed and relaxed as the night carries on. The waitress keeps us supplied with drinks and food, checking on us every so often. Eventually, we decide to call it a night. I mean, we did all work a twelve-hour shift today. We pay and leave Amber, the waitress, a hefty tip. I wave goodbye to Wrenn and head out the door with my new friends. Harriet packs everyone except Elodie into her car.

"Are you sure you don't want a ride?" Harriet asks.

"My girlfriend is on her way but thank you." Elodie assures them. I decide to wait with her. It's barely nine p.m. but I'd never leave a woman behind. Did she mean girlfriend like *girlfriend* or just as a friend? I hate that there isn't a universal subtle way to say *I'm gay* without saying it.

"Do you guys do weekly drinks out?" I ask hopefully.

"We do and we'd love to have you join us next time, too. Here, give me your phone and I'll add you to the group chat." Elodie takes my phone from me.

She notices the background; a photo of me and some friends from college at a pride event last year.

"It's so nice to have another queer friend in the group." She smiles and hands me back my phone. I let out a sigh of relief. You never know how something like that could go.

"Are you...?" I raise an eyebrow.

"Oh, yes. I love women. Super gay over here. My girlfriend is on her way. " She laughs.

"Same here."

"Some of the girls are too but I'll let them disclose who's what." Elodie smiles. "Are you out?"

"Yes. I haven't brought it up at work but it's not a secret for me."

"Gotcha." Elodie nods.

"Babe!" A blue car pulls up and lightly honks her horn at Elodie.

"Erica, this is my new friend Gemma." Elodie introduces me while she gets in the passenger side. She kisses her girlfriend briefly and smiles at me.

"Do you need a ride, Gemma?" Erica asks.

"No, my car is here and I'm perfectly sober, but thank you." I smile.

"See you at work!" Elodie waves goodbye, and I walk to my car alone.

NINE

Norah

"Good morning, Sutton." I smile when I walk into work.

"Good morning, boss." She winks.

"Busy today?" I look around and see more people than usual in the store.

"Yeah, the town's having their annual summer carnival." Sutton looks at me with wide eyes and a tilted head, like how could I forget that.

"Oh yeah." I nod. Pregnancy brain has me forgetting my own name. But that isn't something I can explain.

Sutton heads to the register to help some customers, so I grab some books from the back and start restocking. I only get as far as one aisle when a customer stops me to help them find a book. Which turns into three more before I can find where I left my stack of books. I'm picking it back up when I catch a smell. It's rank, like fresh seafood or something. Whatever it is, I don't have time to investigate it because I'm running to the bathroom.

"Norah?!" Sutton calls after me, but I don't have time to answer.

I make it *just* in time. I spill the contents of my stomach into the toilet, locking the stall behind me. I end up throwing up four times. I'm seeing tiny stars in the corners of my eyes, and I feel dizzy from the straining. Fuck. I know I'm one of the lucky ones who have only gotten sick once so far, and I was hoping to keep it that way. I groan and get sick again. There's a light tap on the door and then someone walks in.

"Um, Norah?" It's Sutton.

"I'm fine," I lie.

"There are a ton of customers. I'm going to call someone to come in." She hesitates. "Do you have your phone if you need me?" She sighs.

"Yes." I feel pathetic. I'm sitting on the floor of the bathroom that is questionably clean.

"Should I stay with you? I'm afraid to leave you alone."

"No, help the customers. I'll be out...*soon*," I say hopefully.

Sutton closes the door behind her, and I dry heave. God, why does this feel so awful? Is my nose connected to my stomach or something? I appreciate that Sutton cares, but there is nothing she can do for me. She's better off helping the store and then calling in a replacement for me. I hate that I can't be more helpful. But if I feel this terrible now, there is no guaranteeing I'll feel any better soon. I pick myself up off the ground and wipe my mouth off with some toilet paper. I don't know how long I've been sitting on the floor, but it feels like forever. When I stand, I'm a little dizzy, but I manage to keep my balance. I'm about to open the stall when I hear the door open again.

"Norah?" That isn't Sutton's voice.

"Mama Perry?" I ask, surprised.

"Oh, yes honey it's me."

I walk out of the stall and find my mother-in-law standing in front of me.

"What are you doing here?" I ask, confused.

"Sutton called me and said I'm your emergency contact." She looks at me with kind eyes. I know what she's saying without saying it. She's touched I put her down for something as important as that.

"She didn't need to call you, I'm okay. Really," I lie as I wash my hands.

"She said you got sick. Do you need me to take you to the doctor?" Despite being in her 60s, she still has her dark hair gray free.

"No, I think it was just some food poisoning. I went out yesterday and should've been more careful with my leftovers," I lie casually. That's believable, right? It's not like she'd automatically assume I'm pregnant.

"Well, at least let me give you a ride home."

"You don't—"

"I insist," she says giving me a look. When she gives you *the look*, you know it isn't optional.

I nod and follow her out of the bathroom.

"I'm going to grab my things from the office," I tell her. She nods and I find Sutton on the phone behind the desk.

"Hi! Are you okay? Sarah is coming in for a shift. Please just go home and rest. I hope it's okay I called someone for you. I didn't want you driving home alone," Sutton blurts out.

"Thank you. I don't work until next week, so I'm hoping to be back by then."

"Of course! Take your time." She smiles. The bell on the door chimes so she disappears to help the customer.

Mama Perry isn't like most mother in-laws. She had welcomed me into the family with open arms. She attended both my parents' funerals, baked me loads of lasagnas and casseroles for the weeks to come, and checked in on me every day. For the last ten years she's been like a mother to me. It was the hardest on both of us when Finn died. We comforted each other and spent time together after. I still go to her house at least once a month for family dinners. So it was hard on me not to tell her that I'm pregnant. But I know I can't get through another loss with her. We're almost in the safety zone. Maybe after twelve weeks I'll have enough courage to tell her. But part of me worries something could still go wrong. There aren't any guarantees.

"I know you're staying with Alana, but I'm not quite sure where that is," Mama Perry says as we get to her car.

"I'm actually staying there with a roommate. Alana is living with her fiancé," I explain.

"Ah," She nods. I put in the address to her phone, and she checks that I'm wearing my seatbelt.

Mama Perry asked me to move in with her before I had decided to live on the Lovers Estate, but I had said no. I thought that if I moved in there, I might never heal. It would be too easy to spend all my time thinking about Finn. As much as I wanted to, I knew I needed to grieve in a healthy way which included moving on in some ways. She understood, as she always did, but I know it disappointed her.

"If you need to get sick, I have garbage bags in the glove box."

"Thank you, I think I'm okay now. I just definitely want to lie down."

"Of course." She smiles.

Five minutes later, we're pulling into my driveway. I'm not surprised when Mama Perry insists on coming in to put me to bed. She's nothing if not thorough. I lead her to my bedroom and excuse myself to use the bathroom. I'm dying to brush my teeth, and of course, pee again. When I come out, she's holding the wedding photo of Finn and I that I keep on my nightstand.

"You were such a beautiful bride." She smiles, placing the frame back down.

"Thank you for coming today; it means a lot to me."

"You're still family to me, sweetheart. It's nice to know you think of me the same way." She smiles.

"I'll save the hugs for when I feel better."

She nods and I climb into bed. She pulls the covers over me and kisses my forehead.

"Do you want me to stay with you, just in case?"

"No, I promise I'm okay. If I need anything else, I'll call you."

"Okay. I'll lock the door behind me."

I shut my eyes when I hear the doors close. I wish I had the courage to tell her the truth. I hope she'll be happy—even if this is an unconventional way of doing things. She's going to be this baby's grandma, and I know Finn would've wanted her as involved as possible.

I fall asleep thinking about Finn and the baby.

"Holy shit. I'm so sorry. I didn't know you were home, but I heard snoring, and it was freaking me out!" Gemma yells as she opens my bedroom door.

"What time is it?"

"Just after five. I just got home from work. But your car wasn't in the driveway. I thought we had a goldilocks situation." She laughs to lighten the mood.

"I went home from work early. I...uh...had food poisoning, so I've been in bed since," I explain.

"Oh, shit. Are you okay? Do you need anything?"

"No, I'm okay. I probably should've warned you my car would be missing, but I didn't think about it." I sit up in bed.

"No, please. I just wanted to make sure everything's okay. I'll let you rest."

"Thank you." I was going to get up and eat something, but the thought of food right now is making me more nauseous.

Gemma closes the door behind her, and I lay my head back down. I grab an applesauce pouch from the drawer in my nightstand and decide to choke it down. There's nothing in my stomach, and as much as food is repulsing me, I need something. I sip on my water lightly, careful not to drink too much too fast. I feel a little bit better, so I pick up my phone and look at my missed messages.

> Mama Perry: Checking in, hope you're okay. When you feel up to it, I'll bring you some homemade chicken noodle soup.
>
> Sutton: Hope you're doing okay!

I text them both back quickly and then put my phone back down. The brightness of the screen is making me a little nauseous right now—even on the lowest setting.

I close my eyes and think about the baby. Something new occurs to me. Well, not new, but it seems more urgent than before. I'm living in someone else's house while I'm about to have a baby. I know Alana wouldn't care if I brought a baby here, but I don't want to be living in someone else's house forever. The baby and I need to be able to have our own space. I need to find a more permanent place for the two of us to live. It isn't ideal to move while pregnant, but I can hire movers.

I know I want to stay in Lovers. Finn and I always talked about raising our kids here, and I like that his family is here. I just need a new place to do it. For the same reason I sold the house Finn and I bought when we got married, I can't be in a home with his ghost. The baby is going to know about him, but I don't want to live in constant reminders of the past. Plus, it isn't like the two of us need an entire house to live in. We'd be happy in an apartment with our own bedrooms.

As soon as I feel better, I need to start apartment hunting. It might take months to find a place. Plus, there are so many things associated with moving. I'll need to find a place, paint and furnish it, and then actually move in. The whole process could take up to a year itself, and I'm on a ticking clock here. I don't want this baby to get used to one space only to move out of it while it's still little. That would be confusing to anyone, especially a baby, right?

I sigh, turning over in bed. I place a hand on my stomach and try to relax. There are so many things I need to do and so many things I can't control. But I can't just sit around and stress about each one. If Finn were here, he'd tell me to take a deep breath and relax. All that stress isn't good for anyone, he'd tell me. I close my eyes and it's almost like he's here in bed with me. I take deep breaths until I'm fast asleep.

TEN

Gemma

Norah has food poisoning for two days and barely leaves her room. I try not to bother her, but I still text her once a day to make sure she's alive in there. I mean...I can hear her throwing up, but I don't want her to know that. So I check in, just in case there's anything I can do for her. She usually says no, but I ask anyway. On the third day, she finally comes out of her bedroom. Not that I was keeping track, but it was nice to see her again. Plus, her car is magically back in the driveway even though I know she didn't leave the house.

"Hey!" I smile but Norah jumps, not expecting to see me in the kitchen.

"Sorry, I thought you were at work." She pulls her robe tight over her waist.

"No worries, I'm off today," I explain.

"Ah, okay." She nods. "I was looking for something that wouldn't hurt my stomach."

"Do you want help?"

"Maybe. Do you know what we have in here, so I don't have to look around?"

"Sure, let me think." I pause. I don't know what to do for an upset stomach. "Whenever I was sick as a kid, my mom would make pasta with butter and some parmesan cheese."

"That sounds delicious." She moans.

"Why don't I help make it?" I suggest.

"I'm fine. I can make some pasta."

"Please, it's not like I'm doing anything," I insist. She hesitates and then nods, taking a seat at the counter.

I grab the pot from the counter and start filling it up with water. Then, I grab a box of noodles from the cabinet. We only have elbow pasta so hopefully that will be okay with her. While I'm cooking the noodles, I grab her a fresh glass of water. For me, I grab a glass of red wine. I'm in the mood for a glass, and I don't have work in the morning. I assume she doesn't want to talk since she's quiet. I don't know if talking would make it worse for her.

"Do you want a plate or a bowl?" I ask.

"A bowl."

I grab two bowls and put them on the counter. Norah watches as I drain the pasta and toss in the melted butter. I pour us each a bowlful and grab two forks and slide the bowl toward Norah.

"You can eat in your room if you want; I know you're not feeling well."

"It's okay, but maybe I don't have to talk?"

"Sure." I nod.

Norah slides the noodles into her mouth and smiles. I'm glad I thought of making it. I sip my wine and stab some elbows onto my fork. It's almost as good as my mother used to make. Norah's still quiet but every so often she looks up and smiles at me. Her white teeth stare back at me and my lips curve. Even like this, sick as can be, she manages to look beautiful. Her red hair is in a tight bun, and she's finally getting some of the color back in her cheeks. I watch her carefully, wishing I could look away. My crush on her grows each time I hang out with her.

"Thank you for dinner." Norah finishes up and puts her bowl

in the sink. She disappears into her room, and I clean up the dishes.

Every night after dinner, I've been reading in the spare room. It's been lonely without Norah, but it's still comfortable and cozy in there. So I change into my pajamas and then grab my Kindle and a blanket. I settle into the couch that's next to the window. I'm looking out the window when Norah walks into the room with an armful of her stuff.

"Oh." She frowns. "You're in my spot."

"Don't worry! There's room for you." I pat the couch space next to me.

"I probably shouldn't. I don't know if I'm over the...stomach bug." She frowns.

"Ah okay." I nod.

Norah curls up in a ball in the corner of the other couch. Her blanket is draped over her, and the color is fully back in her cheeks now. Once she's settled, I ask her what she's going to read.

"I'm on the last chapter of this book for book club. It's called *Out on a Limb* by Hannah Bonam-Young." She smiles.

"You're in a book club?"

"Yeah, the bookstore I work at hosts one. It's once a month on the second Tuesday of the month," she explains.

"Ah. Is it a big group?"

"Not really, it's like me and three others." She pauses. "You should come join us."

"I didn't read the book."

"Well, we have snacks and talk about books in general. And there's wine."

"Maybe next month? If you tell me the book?"

"Sure, we'll pick it on Tuesday night."

"Do you always read the same genre?"

"Mainly romance, but sometimes we switch it up."

"I finished the Sara Cate series, by the way. I'm SO pissed that book four doesn't come out until next year." I sigh.

"You know it's always worth it."

"That's true," I agree.

"Do you have work tomorrow?"

"No, I'm off. How about you?"

"I don't work again until Monday. My boss gave me off to make sure I'm over being sick," she says.

"That's good at least."

"Yeah, I just hope I feel better tomorrow enough to at least go outside. I hate being in the house so many days."

"Are you an extrovert then?"

"I think so. I'm definitely more of a people and outside person. I don't mind staying inside, but after a few days I go stir crazy."

"Well, we can't have that." I laugh.

"After my, uh…husband passed away, I didn't leave the house for two weeks. Just the funeral and then home until my mother-in-law made me go for a walk."

"Did that help?" I'm surprised because this is the first time she's ever talked about her husband before.

"Sort of. More just being around her helped. She's not, like, a stereotypical mother-in-law. She's great."

"Do you still see her?"

"I do. She lives in town, so we have dinner together sometimes." She smiles as I nod.

Apparently neither of us know what to say next, so Norah picks up her book, an actual book, and I turn on my Kindle. I'm just starting a new book series that someone in my reading group recommended, so I'm excited to see if I enjoy it. I'm glad Norah is back to feeling well enough to read in here. Her presence was definitely missed when she wasn't feeling well.

The more I learn about Norah, the more I like her. It is *silly*. She had a *husband*. Alana said she'd only dated men. She's more than likely straight. And you know the number one rule: don't fall for straight girls. She's so more than just a beautiful face, though. She's kind and smart, and we have *so* much in common.

Maybe it's just because I'm a little bit lonely. It's been so long since I dated or even hooked up with anyone. Maybe this is just my body's way of telling me to get back out there. Whatever it is, I don't appreciate her being all I can think about while I'm trying to read. She's going to think I was some creeper if I keep looking at her.

I try to distract myself with my book. It's a romance I'm not paying much attention to, but it isn't the book's fault. I'm just focused on Norah today. I hate that I missed her when she was sick. I know that I shouldn't—this crush is and will always be one-sided. But it isn't like I can stop it from happening. I force myself to pay attention to the single mom in my book and read as the brute bartender falls for her.

All of a sudden, I hear a low snore. My head snaps up, and I realize Norah's passed out on the other couch with her book in her hands. Her mouth hangs open lightly, and she snores again. I smile to myself. She must be exhausted from being sick. I pick up my things, deciding to give her a little privacy to sleep. I stop to pull her blanket over her and turn off her book. She moves slightly but doesn't wake up. I turn on the lamp and switch off the overhead light. I don't know if she'll wake or not, but she doesn't need so much light on her. I leave the door open and head for my room. On the way there, my phone starts vibrating in my pocket.

"Hello?" I pick up the phone without looking to see who it was. No one calls me unless it's important.

"Well look who finally picked up the phone," my mom scolds from the other end of the phone.

"Hi, mom." I smile. Settling into my room, I close my bedroom door behind me.

"I thought you were going to call when you got in! It's been weeks since you got there."

"I know, I've been working a lot. I'm sorry. How are you?"

"Better now that I've gotten ahold of you." She's so dramatic. I know for a fact she hasn't tried to call me before this.

"What's going on?" I ask.

"Nothing here, but I wanted to check in on you. How's the job? The place? How's Alana doing?" My mother adores Alana and will be making an appearance at the wedding come the end of the summer.

"The house is beautiful—way nicer than any of the usual places they put me up at. The job is great. I went out with some co-workers already. This town is so small and cute, but I like it here. Alana is doing well, just pre-wedding stress but nothing to worry about."

"Oh, I'm so glad you're making friends! It makes me feel so much better about you traveling all the time." I'm a few years away from thirty, and my mother acts like I'm a spinster in my eighties.

"How are Phil and Liz doing?" I ask about my stepdad and baby sister. Well, she's twenty-one, but to me, she'll always be my baby sister.

"Phil is great! We go to the club and swim during the week. Your sister finally agreed to sign up for classes at UConn, so hopefully that'll motivate her. I don't know what to do with her, she's not motivated like you and your brother were."

"Give her some time, she's just not sure what she wants to do yet. But she has time."

"I guess, I just don't want her sleeping on my couch for the next twenty years." My mom sighs.

"She won't. She might be on mine, if I ever settle down." I laugh.

"Oh, please. Tell me you're at least dating. Have Alana introduce you to a nice woman. It can't hurt to meet someone."

"I'm only here for a few months."

"Yes, but you could always stay."

"You think I'll find someone worth sticking around for?" I ask, unconvinced.

"Why not? It could happen."

"Sure," I say just to appease my mom. It isn't that I don't

believe her. The issue is that the only person who comes to mind is Norah. And I need to stop myself from even going there.

"What's the latest gossip?" I ask, knowing it'll take the attention off me. My mom *loves* to gossip. She lives in the same small town in Connecticut where I grew up, and she often has updates about my old classmates.

My mom goes on and on about who's married and who just found out they're expecting, and I breathe a sigh of relief. I appreciate that my mom cares so much, and she's supportive of whoever I want to be with. But I don't want the pressure of trying to find my forever person right now.

ELEVEN

Gemma

"Thanks for inviting me. I know the hospital does this every year, but I've never been to one." Norah smiles. She has her red hair tied back with a pink ribbon that matches the pink in her sundress. Her freckles are more prominent today in the sun—as are her green eyes.

"Thank you for being a buffer. I didn't want to be a third wheel with Alana and Will." I smile. I can't let on to Norah about how Will and I don't get along.

He was a last-minute invite when his business trip got cancelled, and he just *had* to come along with Alana. I knew I couldn't say no, and it was the perfect reason to invite Norah along too. At least some good came out of him going.

"Norah! Gemma!" Alana calls out and waves us over to the picnic tables.

We're all set up on the grounds right outside the hospital. There are rides, games, food trucks, and picnic tables for the festival. Alana and Will are holding hands, but both look overly dressed for the day. Alana is wearing a name brand pantsuit while Will looks like he just got off a yacht. I once saw Alana do a keg stand in a bikini, so to see her like this is *weird*. It feels almost unnatural.

"Thanks for inviting us. I love this kind of stuff." Alana smiles.

"It's quite interesting to see," Will muses and looks around trying to hide his distaste.

"I did my shift at the fair booth earlier, so I'm glad you guys are here now. We can grab some food or do some rides."

"Yes! Let's ride something. Norah?" Alana looks at her friend.

"Oh, no thanks. I don't do rides."

"What about high school when you rode the gravitron six times and beat Tyler when he thought he could outnumber you?" Alana asks, shocked.

"I'm old now, dude, no rides for me." Norah chuckles lightly.

"Don't worry, I don't like rides either." I smile. I had seen them put together this morning and none of them looked safe. Let's just say I was relieved the hospital was ten feet away.

"Fine. Will can come with me. Won't you?" Alana gives him a pout and puppy dog eyes.

"Of course." He makes a big show of buying way too many tickets to *support the community* when in reality, I think he just wants to brag about his wealth.

Will and Alana disappear to try out a few different rides, leaving Norah and I alone.

"Food?" I raise an eyebrow.

"Yes please." She groans.

Something I've learned about Norah is how much she enjoys food. She's not just someone who eats because she has to...she eats food she genuinely enjoys. Plus, she eats such an open variety of food. I never know what she's cooking or going to come home with. Norah always seems to be snacking on something too. She must work out a lot or just has a crazy good metabolism because you could not tell how she eats by looking at her.

We walk over to the food trucks together in silence despite the sounds of the crowds around us. Kids are screaming, rides are making noises, music is playing from a variety of booths. I follow her to the deep-fried Oreo booth and watch in amazement as she orders three orders just for herself. I order myself one and then we start to walk back to the rides to find Alana and Will. We both take an Oreo out of the bag and a poof of powdered sugar rushes in my face. I quickly wipe it off as Norah quietly giggles.

"Read anything good lately?" Between work and her not being home, it has been a few nights since we've read together.

"I was reading a really beautiful poetry collection on grief, actually."

"Was it helpful?"

"I think so; it wasn't focused on letting go as much as others usually are. This one was just about reliving the good moments and soaking in all of the person you lost."

"I think that's lovely." I smile.

"Finn, my husband. I think that's how he would've wanted things. For me to relive the good but also live my life."

"He probably loved you as much as you love him, so I'm sure he didn't want you to let go or hold on either. The middle that you seem to have found is good."

"Exactly. I didn't mean to bring up…well, death. But it's nice sometimes to talk about it with someone who didn't know me before. You're not waiting for me to go back to who I was like it seems some people are," Norah admits.

"I think people just don't know how to handle grief. I'm definitely no expert, but as long as you're taking care of you then you have to do what works." I shrug.

Norah nods and takes another Oreo in her mouth. This time she somehow ends up with a bit on her nose. Without thinking, I reach forward to wipe it off. My thumb touches her nose lightly and she looks at me curiously. Her green eyes searching my face for something. My mouth goes dry as I think of something to say.

"Gemma!" Alana's voice calls out, and Norah and I jump apart.

"Yes?" I turn around, forcing a smile on my face. My best friend didn't mean to ruin a moment.

"We've been looking for you guys. We did like three rides and then a kid almost puked on Will." She laughs.

"Hey, that was so not funny," Will says in a warning tone.

"Well, it was to me." Alana giggles. She reaches into the bag and steals one of my deep friend Oreos.

"Oh sure, help yourself," I say sarcastically.

"No problem!" Alana smiles and manages to get powdered sugar all over her lips.

She pulls Will in for a kiss and wipes the powdered sugar all over his cheek. While playfully fun to Alana, Will turns bright red in anger and stomps away without another word. Alana's cheeks turn pink as she realizes what she did. She brushes off the rest of the remains and runs after Will. Norah and I stay frozen in our spots, unsure of if we should go after them.

"I think we should wait here," she says as if reading my mind.

"Is he really that mad?" I frown. It was a harmless joke.

"Probably." Norah sighs.

"Something to share?" I raise an eyebrow.

"Not really. Just that she seems to always be apologizing for being herself. Like that was a harmless moment to me, if anything it looked like something out of a cheesy rom-com. But anytime she does something like that, Will freaks out," Norah explains.

"Yeah, that's not the first time."

I turn to see Alana and Will yelling at each other across the festival. They're both talking with their arms and gesturing things. I have no idea what they're saying, but neither of them looks happy. Will might've gotten a little sugar on his shirt, but it wasn't like it was going to stain. I hate seeing how Alana lets him get away with everything.

"Can we play a game?" Norah asks. She tosses the empty bag

of Oreos in the garbage and squirts her hands with some hand sanitizer.

"Sure, any in mind?" I tear myself away from the drama unfolding before me.

"I wanna do a ring toss! I've never been any good so I'm sure I'll end up donating lots of money," Norah says proudly.

"Ring toss it is." I laugh.

I lead the way to the ring toss booth, and sure enough, Norah was right: she sucks. She is tossing rings all over the place but not getting it on a single bottle. But no one could say she isn't having fun trying. With each ring, she has a hopeful smile on her face no matter how badly she threw the last one. Plus, she's willing to buy more and more rings. I'm not sure if she's determined to win or she just wants to donate to the hospital. Either way, it's fun to watch. She finally calls it quits after at least $100 spent.

"I have to pee, I'll be right back," she informs me. I decide to stay put and wait for her.

"Want a shot? Win your girl a prize?" The guy hosting the booth is one of the doctors. I don't remember his name, but I like that he called Norah my girl. Even if she isn't...even if no one heard it.

"Sure." I take out five dollars and he hands me three rings.

The first ring is close but falls behind the bottles, the second makes it on and everyone cheers, and the last one falls to the floor. I laugh.

"Pick any prize from the first row," he tells me, and I pick out the small giraffe. I don't really know why, but it looks like something Norah would like.

Ten minutes later, Norah comes back holding two large cups of lemonade.

"They had a lemonade booth right next to the bathrooms, which is smart honestly. But it looked so good I got you one." She smiles.

"I won you this." I hold out the giraffe to her, and her eyes light up.

"No way! On the ring toss?! I thought that thing was rigged! You'll have to show me one day how you beat it. Thank you so much, Gemma. I love it." She gushes and my heart swells. Something about this girl saying my name makes butterflies appear.

"Thanks for the lemonade." I sip it quickly, hoping to contain my blush.

"Oh, what do we name him?" She holds up the little giraffe proudly.

"What about Raf?"

"Raf the giraffe? I love it." She giggles and tucks him under her arm.

"We should probably go find Alana, see if she's okay," I suggest.

"Sounds good to me." Norah nods.

We walk toward the parking lot hoping to find Alana, and we end up finding her next to Norah's car. She's got her arms crossed over her chest, and she's alone. She does not look happy to say the least. At least it isn't aimed at us.

"Where's Will?" I ask, looking around. I have a feeling I already know the answer.

"He left me here. Well, I told him to leave me here. If he wants to be a grump about stupid shit then he can just go home," Alana grumbles.

"Do you need a ride home?" Norah asks.

"I was hoping I can stay with you guys tonight. I do not want to go home, but I don't want to make a thing about it and tell anyone else," she explains.

"Of course. There's literally three other bedrooms we never even use." I laugh.

"Not to mention, it's yours," Norah adds lightly.

"I left my car in the staff parking lot, so I'll meet you both at home?"

They both nod, and I head in the opposite direction to get my car. I feel bad for Alana. This looks more and more like she and Will just don't work as a couple and less like pre wedding jitters —or whatever nonsense she tries calling it. I don't want her to make a big mistake and marry someone who makes her feel like this. She should be marrying someone who laughs when she wipes powdered sugar on them and loves all the little parts of her. I know tonight isn't the night to say anything, but if this kind of thing continues, I know I'll need to say something. She's one of my best friends. I refuse to stand next to her on her wedding day without knowing I've been completely honest with her. And without knowing she's happy and completely sure of who she's marrying.

TWELVE

Norah

The more time I spend with Gemma, the more confused I am. I've always thought I'm strictly into men, more specifically, Finn. He was my high school sweetheart. We got married young, and I always thought that would be it. I had never considered there would be anyone else—man or woman. I don't know if it's the new hormones, not that I think being pregnant could turn you gay. But there must be some sort of an explanation, right? Because all of a sudden, my fantasies and thoughts are wrapped up in *her*.

This is how, on more than one occasion, I've found myself googling how late in life people can realize they're gay. I guess coming out later in life is more common than I once thought, because there are tons of articles and posts and groups about people coming out in their thirties, forties, fifties, and so on. I'm not even thirty yet, so am I even truly a late bloomer? And what does it all mean? A lot of my friends are into women, so it isn't something new to me. Still, I never noticed other women the way they did.

I had *Finn*. I noticed *Finn*.

Now suddenly, I'm *noticing* Gemma. The way she smiles with her lips closed and a dimple forms on the right side of her cheek.

The way she laughs with her whole body and makes everyone in the room laugh too. The way she listens to me no matter what we're talking about and really thinks before responding. How she always makes sure to take the time to consider my feelings. She's beautiful, I noticed that right away, but all these little things suddenly make it feel like *more*.

I've fantasized about her on more than one occasion. Usually Finn is there too, but lately it's more of us being alone…also a new feeling for me. Is this just part of my grieving process? Attaching to someone new and nearby? It doesn't feel like a new step in the grief process, it feels *different*. Gemma and I spend nearly every night together talking about books, our lives… everything. Most of the time we bring our Kindles and books, but we hardly ever use them at this point.

According to the gay test I took—yes, I actually took one. It's possible I'm more pansexual: I'm attracted to the person rather than what parts they may or may not have. It makes sense to me. I was attracted to Finn, and now I'm attracted to Gemma. It's simple.

Except, it isn't. I can't do a damn thing about it. I'm nearly done with my first trimester, and that's no place to be starting a new relationship with someone. Sure, I'm almost done puking my guts out, but a relationship? I don't even know if I'm ready for something like that in general.

I pull out the box I keep under my bed and open the lid. I open the sealed envelope and pull out some of the love notes Finn wrote me. When we first started dating, he wrote them to me all the time. Then it became less frequent, only getting them on birthdays and anniversaries. He hand wrote each one and sprayed them all with his cologne. I put the note to my nose and inhale. Closing my eyes, it's like he's in the room with me. His warm scent envelops my senses and I feel at ease.

When I miss him or I just want to remember him, I pull out a letter or two and read them. It often makes me feel a little better. Sometimes I cry, but it's always for the better. I pull out two random ones and put the rest back in the box. I re-read his terrible handwritten notes—his handwriting was like a toddler with a crayon. But his words are what matter. The tears pour down my cheeks, and I read them.

When I'm done, I put them away and put the box under my bed. I place my hand on my stomach and focus on my breathing. My therapist taught me how to mediate in the early days of losing Finn. Back when I had daily appointments just to get me out the door. I count in for three, hold for three, and breathe out for three. I do this a few times over until I feel relaxed. It's still too early to feel the baby in my belly, but I like having my hand there. Maybe the baby can feel that, who knows?

"Hey, Norah?" Gemma knocks on my door. I sit up and fold my shirt back over my stomach.

"Yes?" I call, and she opens the door.

"I was wondering if you want to do something with me tomorrow?" Gemma smiles. She looks sort of anxious; she's twirling her fingers in her hands.

"Sure. I don't have work." I smile.

"Would you like to take a boat ride with me? I've been dying to see the lighthouse from the water."

"Yeah, that sounds great."

"Perfect, it's a date." Gemma spins around and closes the door behind her.

I'm about to throw up. Did Gemma just use the word date? But she didn't mean it like a real date, right? She just meant it like the way people joke and say *it's a date*. Gemma doesn't know I'm having these feelings for her, does she? I don't think I've been obvious but then again, I don't know exactly what these feelings are. Oh, no. I'm freaking out again. It isn't that I don't want to go out with Gemma; it's the fact that I *really* want to.

"Are you okay?" Sutton asks, startling me out of my daze.

"What?" I look at her confused.

"You seem a little out of it lately. Is anything going on?" She raises an eyebrow.

I hesitate. Up until this point, I've been pretty open with Sutton. She knows all about Finn and everything I went through. It isn't a secret, and I enjoy talking to her about things. But I'm just ready for anyone else to know about the baby, not yet. So instead, I share the other reason I was mentally freaking out today.

"Remember how Alana's maid of honor moved in in the beginning of last month?"

"Sure, you said she's cool."

"She sort of asked me on a date…I think." I wrinkle my eyebrows together.

"Oh my goodness!" Sutton squeals, and I shush her, pulling her into a random row of books in the store. It was a pretty quiet day, so it wasn't like we were ignoring anyone by not working.

"What does this mean? Are you considering it? Are you into women like that? I have *so* many questions," Sutton gushes, and I don't know how to answer any of her questions.

"I—I don't know," I admit.

"Okay, basics. Are you attracted to her?"

"Yes, I think so." I nod.

"Okay, and you say she *sort of* asked you on a date? What exactly does that mean?"

"She asked me to go on a boat ride with her tomorrow and when I said yes, she smiled and said *it's a date*," I explain.

"Hmm, that's a tough one. Like it totally could be, but then I've also been known to say *it's a date* to friends of mine." Sutton purses her pink lips. "Can you ask her?"

"No, no, no, because I don't know if I want it to be."

"So you aren't sure if you want to go?"

"I'm not sure if I'm ready to date anyone."

"That's completely understandable." She nods.

"But I don't want to lead her on either."

"Yeah, this is a tough one. I'd say see how it goes tomorrow and try to use neutral language. If you don't treat it like a date, then maybe she won't treat it like a date."

"That makes sense, but what if she's already treating it like a date?"

"Then I'd just be honest with her and say you aren't ready for that. You like her but you're still grieving and maybe in the future it's something you can revisit?"

"That isn't too harsh?"

"Norah, you lost your husband. Anyone who doesn't understand that isn't someone you should waste your time with." She has a good point.

"Excuse me? Could someone help me please?" A person peeks around the corner of the shelves we're standing in, but I recognize it as Emery, Sutton's best friend.

"Hey! What are you doing here?!" Sutton squeals and slides into her best friend's arms for a hug.

"I got out of work early, so I thought I'd come surprise you." Emery smiles.

"I'll be in the office if you need me. Nice to see you again, Emery," I excuse myself to give them some time to chat.

There isn't much to do, and it isn't any different than the chatting we were just doing. In the office I can at least sit down and get some of the payroll for the week done. It isn't technically my job, but it keeps me busy, and I like that.

But as I pull up the payroll, my mind is on Gemma again. Maybe I'm just overthinking it. I mean, it isn't like she asked me to be her girlfriend or some crazy thing that was way too soon. She just asked me to hang out, probably in a platonic way, for all I know. Part of me just wishes it might be more. As much as that absolutely terrifies me. I try to focus on the paperwork, checking and double-checking hours to make sure everyone gets paid what they're supposed to. It's a simple job at times like this when it's only a few employees. There isn't too much room for error, considering we mostly work the same shifts every week. But still, I double check just to make sure there are no errors.

My phone goes off in my pocket, and I slide it out to see it's the baby bump app I had downloaded weeks earlier. It goes off every day and tells me facts about the baby, my body, and the size of the baby. It's a cute way to remind me that this is real and I'm not sick to my stomach for no reason. I unlock my phone and click on the app. I'm officially twelve weeks along today, which means I'm officially out of the woods and about to start my second trimester. Not that a million other things couldn't go wrong, but according to my doctor and the app, this is the time when people start to announce things—which of course scares the crap out of me. I don't even know where to begin or who to tell.

It was never my intention to keep this baby a secret, but to think about the fact that I'm going to be bombarded with a million and two questions…it scares me. I look at the app and it tells me the baby is the size of a lime today. Now I have the urge to stop by the grocery store on the way home and pick one up just to see. It's hard to imagine that there's a small person just growing inside me while I live my life out here. I read over the symptoms I might experience and wince. They always try to make it sound like it won't be so bad when they're literally talking about farting more or peeing less.

Maybe once I feel a little more secure in my pregnancy, I'll start telling my friends. Heather already knows and checks in on me all the time. I don't want to tell Alana this close to the wedding, especially with how much stress she's under. But maybe the rest of my friends can keep a secret. It isn't like I'm asking them to keep it from her forever, and she'll understand…

I hope.

THIRTEEN

Gemma

Somehow, I let the words "it's a date" slip from my mouth, and it's been haunting me ever since. Norah went to work shortly after I talked to her, and I've been pacing the house like an idiot instead of catching up on my rest like I should be. Why did I have to go on and say it was a date? I could've just let things be and had a nice day with her. But no, I had to be stupid and add that word which adds way too much pressure. I don't know if it's obvious or not that I like her, but it sure is obvious now. I mean, sure she said yes, but is she going to come home and cancel because I tacked on such a silly word? I'm pacing around the living room and the kitchen and to my room and back. I need to get some sleep. I should *definitely* get some sleep.

I force myself to take a long, hot shower hoping the steam and the hot water will calm me down and force me to relax. But of course, it doesn't. So I sneak one of Norah's teas and sip it in bed while I read on my Kindle. I'm used to sleeping when everyone else is still awake, but my nerves have me all messed up today. I finally shut off my Kindle and all the lights and turn on the TV, playing *Twilight* in the background. It comforts me enough to do the trick and force me to close my eyes and relax a little bit.

When I wake up, it's because of the sun shining in my face and Norah is knocking lightly at my door. I make sure my boobs are in my tank top and not wilding out before answering the door. Norah's standing before me with a cup of tea in hand and still in her pajamas. They're a matching set of flannel that I'm wondering how she's wearing in the summer. But I guess it is cool in here with the AC on.

"Hi, I was just wondering what time you wanted to leave." She smiles.

"Oh, I set up the boat for noon. I wasn't sure if you were a morning person or not," I explain.

"Okay, I'm not. But I didn't want to be late. I'll go back to bed and set an alarm." She laughs.

"Perfect." I smile.

"See you later." Norah leaves with the door shut behind her, and my stomach is a zoo of butterflies as I lie back down.

I stare at the tan ceiling as I try to calm myself. Norah is so beautiful, and her voice is always so soft. She reminds me of a Disney princess. Like one of the powerful ones who speaks softly and is kind to everyone and accidentally falls in love with a prince. Every time I think about her, I can't help but smile. I have no clue how I'm going to last spending the day with her. Last time we did I ended up winning her that stuffed giraffe and spending the night consoling Alana with her. Alana got drunk on red wine and threw up on the couch and then cried in the shower. She was a mess, but Norah and I took care of her until the morning. Once Alana had fallen asleep, we stayed awake as long as we could because we didn't want to stop talking.

Surprisingly, I fall back asleep and wake up an hour later.

This time I get up and get dressed. I toss on a cute pair of overalls and a T-shirt with a pair of sneakers. The weather said it was supposed to be nice and hot today, so I pack my bathing suit just in case we decide to go swimming. I know Norah can swim since she spent two summers lifeguarding as a teenager. I pack a bag of all the essentials, brush my teeth, and head to the kitchen.

Norah is lounging on the couch, reading a novel. Her hair is in a messy top knot, she's chewing on something, and has a bowl next to her. I have to get closer to see that she's munching on a bowl of fresh cherries. She pops them off the stem and then spits the seed out into the bowl. It takes her a minute to realize I'm in the room with her and she almost jumps, clutching the book to her chest.

"Oh my goodness! Don't sneak up on me." She gasps.

"I'm sorry. I didn't mean to scare you." I laugh. I read the title of the book—it's a psychological thriller, of course she's jumpy.

"I have to read this during the day or else I get too scared. But apparently that doesn't work when I'm not paying attention." She laughs, closing the book.

"You'll have to tell me if it's good enough for me to move up on my TBR."

"Definitely, unless the killer is who I think it is. Then no, it's way too obvious."

"Gotcha." I nod.

I head into the kitchen and begin making a quick breakfast. Norah went grocery shopping the day before, and I guess she's on a fruit kick because the fridge is stocked with every fruit imaginable. I decide to make a protein smoothie and look for the blender. Norah follows me into the kitchen, still snacking on her cherries that are painting her lips a delicious red. I clench my jaw, thinking about how much I would love to kiss her right now. God, I bet she tastes as sweet as she looks. She's put her hair down now, the red waves all around her face as she looks up at me.

"There's more cherries in the fridge if you want some." Norah smiles. She must've caught me staring.

"Oh sure." I nod.

"Do you want to pack a lunch?"

"Yeah that's a good idea. I have a cooler in my car that I can bring."

"Perfect. I already made us some sandwiches and packed some snacks, but I didn't have anywhere to put them," she says shyly.

I make the smoothie, switch it to a to-go cup, and grab the cooler out of my car. It's warm to the touch, so I add extra ice for good measure. Norah grabs her bag, and I notice she's got her bathing suit on under her yellow sundress. The green straps show in the back of her pale skin. I'm excited for today, as long as I don't say anything stupid again, we'll have a good day.

I pull into the parking lot near the dock of the boat I rented. I already have the keys, and I was told everything else would be taken care of. My parents had a boat when I was growing up, and although it wasn't exactly legal, my dad had taught me how to drive one. It wasn't too different from driving a car and it was easier on a nice day like today. Norah slides on her dark sunglasses as I pack everything into the boat. I help her aboard, holding her hand which is softer than it looks.

"Where'd you learn how to do this?"

"I'm from Connecticut, so my parents have a lake house, and we had a boat growing up." I hate how rich it makes me sound because yes, my parents have money, but it's not like my money wasn't earned.

"That's awesome. I bet you were popular then."

"Not really, my brother and sister were, though. Do you have any siblings?"

"Nope. Only child." She frowns.

"Siblings aren't all they're cracked up to be. But mine are okay now." I laugh.

"Alana and Wrenn get along much better than they did a decade ago," Norah adds. I nod.

When I feel like we're in a good spot, I stop the boat and join Norah on the deck. We take in the view of the water, the quiet of the waves, and how blue everything looks out here. Norah's looking at the lighthouse, and I can't help but look at her. She's so beautiful, and I wish I was brave enough to tell her so.

"I love coming out here. I can't remember the last time I took a day and just did nothing like this. It's so relaxing." She beams at me.

"Well, anytime you want to go this summer just say the word." I smile. I'm standing close enough that I can smell the cherries she was eating earlier and the shampoo she must use.

A gust of wind blows our hair, and it gets tangled together. We're both in a fit of giggles as we manage to tame our hair and her necklace out from each other. Norah looks at me, and we're both quiet. I stare at her lips once more, begging for her to make the first move. To give me some small sign that this isn't in my head, and she wants this. Norah's lips curve up on the side, and she looks at me expectantly. I take a step closer and her breathing steadies. I watch as her eyes don't leave my face, dancing back and forth between my lips and eyes. I want to say something, but my mouth is unwilling.

Just as our lips are about to press together, Norah turns away and retches. Her stomach emptying over the side of the boat into the water. I pull back her red hair and hold it up as she gets sick. I'm a nurse; it isn't like vomit is disgusting to me. I wait for it to pass, for her to stand up and look at me so I can assess her. Clearly, we need to get back, but I want to make sure she's okay first. She didn't say she had a history of getting seasick and wouldn't that have happened when we first got on the boat? It isn't like the water is suddenly rough or something.

Norah turns around and takes her hair from me, scooping it into a high ponytail. She takes a deep breath and sits on the edge of the boat. She looks pale but not feverish. I touch her forehead with the back of my hand and confirm she doesn't feel hot.

"Do you have any other symptoms?"

"No." She shakes her head.

"Can I get you water?" She nods so I race to the cooler and grab a fresh bottle, opening the cap for her and handing it to her. Norah takes a small sip and smiles.

"I'm sorry."

"No, I'm sorry. I didn't know you get seasick."

"I-I don't."

"Oh, then are you sick again? Is this another virus? Because so many within thirty days you should really get checked by a doctor. There could be something bigger going on."

"I'm fine. But I think I need to get home."

I pause. She's clearly not fine but maybe this is something she doesn't feel comfortable sharing with me. I decide not to press the issue and turn the boat around. I help Norah to the deck and find a bucket she can use as a garbage can in case she gets sick again.

"Sit here. I'm going to get us back to land and then we can decide what to do."

Norah nods and throws up again. I turn on the boat and safely direct us back to shore. We dump the garbage can on the way out, and Norah takes my hand to follow me to the car. She looks a little better since she had some water, but she doesn't seem better. As she takes her time getting in the car, I think about what to say next. Do I just bring her home? Do I call Alana? Do I take her to the hospital? I definitely won't leave her alone, that's for sure.

"There's something I need to tell you," Norah says as she slides into the passenger seat.

FOURTEEN

Norah

It's not embarrassing enough that I get sick on a boat with the girl I like, but I had to do it right as she was about to kiss me. I feel like the biggest idiot in the world.

"What is it?" Gemma looks at me.

"Can you take us home and we can talk there? I'll explain everything. I promise." I look at her for reassurance.

"Okay." She nods.

She takes the quick way home and before I talk to her, I disappear into the bathroom to brush my teeth and wash my face. Once I feel like myself again, I grab a sleeve of crackers from the kitchen and meet Gemma in the spare room. It sort of makes sense; it's like our room.

"Are you okay?" Gemma looks up at me from the couch. I take a seat across from her in my usual spot.

"I am, yes. Thank you. I'm sorry about…"

"I'm a nurse. Trust me when I say I've seen way worse." She waves me off.

"Okay, so I know I've been sick a lot recently, and I probably should've told you sooner, but I didn't really know how. I'm pregnant." I wince involuntarily, waiting for the blowback.

Gemma's eyes look like they're going to pop back into her

head but then she carefully rights herself. I can tell she's trying to do some sort of doctor math based on my symptoms or wondering what the best way to ask me who the father is.

"Okay, so *pregnant*. I guess that makes sense given all the morning sickness." She nods, trying to make sense of it.

"You can ask me anything or I can try to explain, whatever's easier."

Gemma hesitates. "Why don't you explain?"

"Okay." I nod. I try to figure out where to start.

"So when Finn passed, we were in the process of attempting IVF. He didn't want anyone to know at first. He was a proud guy, so he asked that we keep it private. I was actually at the doctor when I got the call that he was going to the hospital. We stopped the procedure and put the embryos on ice. I figured I'd wait until he was better, and we'd try again. But obviously that didn't happen, so I decided that I wanted to be a mom, even if it was going to be on my own. So I used our embryos to get pregnant. I'm about twelve weeks along now. Which is when I can technically tell people, but I've been hesitant to given the situation, so only Heather knows," I explain.

"Wow," Gemma looks at me with wide eyes.

"Yes."

I give Gemma a moment to collect her thoughts. I don't blame her for being surprised. I'm sure the last thing she anticipated was this. Gemma is quiet for a few moments before she speaks.

"I'm so sorry I misread things between us. I never would've tried to kiss you if I didn't think you were interested..." She looks so distraught.

"Please don't apologize."

"No, I'm serious. I should've talked to you first before trying to kiss you. That was a bad move on my part—"

"Gemma, I wanted you to kiss me." I reach for her hand, and she looks at me.

"You did?" Her tone doesn't hide her surprise.

"I did."

"So you're having a baby, and you wanted me to kiss you," Gemma muses as if those are two very normal things to say in a sentence together.

"Well, yeah." I laugh, because if you can't laugh then I don't know what to tell you. "I understand if this changes things for you. This is probably one of the last things you were expecting to hear."

"It was." Gemma purses her lips. "But you like me? You're not straight?"

"I don't think so."

"You don't think so? Can you clarify that?" she adds with a lighthearted chuckle.

"I've never been attracted to a woman before. But I am attracted to and like you. So I don't entirely know what that means."

"Ah, well that makes sense if you've mainly only dated your husband."

"That's true. I never really had the chance to date anyone else, not that I wanted to. I'm just very new to all of this." I motion between us and Gemma smiles.

"That's okay. Everyone figures things out in their own time," she reassures me.

"But that doesn't bother you?"

"I just know that I like you. But I'm not here to make your life more complicated. If you say you have too much going on, then we stay friends and nothing has to change."

"But if I like you too?"

"Then I'm open to seeing where this takes us. At your own pace of course."

I think for a minute. Gemma makes me feel safe and validated in her words. She isn't pushing this or pushing me in any way. It seems like she genuinely wants to see where this takes us but she isn't trying to rush things. She is considering my feelings in every way. Which of course only makes me like her more.

"I think I'd like to see how things go, slowly please," I say aloud.

"Okay." Gemma smiles and looks between our hands and my lips.

I blush. Is she about to kiss me? Thank goodness I brushed my teeth.

"How are you feeling?" she asks.

"I'm all good now. I think it was the boat making me seasick because of the pregnancy. It's never happened to me before," I explain.

"And you're seeing a doctor for the pregnancy, right?"

"Yes. I have an OB and see her every few weeks for a check in and sonograms." I smile.

"Okay, pregnancy is hard on the body. You definitely don't want to skip any appointments or not have a doctor to call just in case."

"I have a good one, and she understands my situation, which is important to me."

"Good." Gemma smiles. "Now, would it be inappropriate to tell you that I'd like to kiss you?"

I laugh. "No, I was sort of thinking the same thing."

"Are you nervous?"

"A little. I've never kissed a girl before." I blush.

"We'll go slow. And if you aren't into it, we'll just stop. No biggie." Gemma shrugs.

"Okay." I stand up to sit next to her on the couch.

Gemma looks at me with the same desire she did on the boat. Her dark brown eyes are on my lips, and I can feel my cheeks burning. It's like my first kiss all over again. Except...I'm not thirteen, and it isn't during a game of spin the bottle. It's just Gemma and I, and it's safe for me to see if I really want this. Even though I have a strong suspicion I do.

Gemma pushes back a loose strand of hair and tucks it behind my ear. She places her open palm on my left cheek and leans in. I close my eyes and pucker my lips ever so slightly.

Hers meet mine in a soft, chaste kiss. She waits for me to say something, but I don't. That was nothing. So she goes in again, this time pressing her lips to mine longer. A shiver runs down my spine, and I can feel the heat burning between my thighs.

"How was that?" Gemma pulls back to ask.

"I think we could keep going," I say peeking open my eyes.

Gemma laughs and leans in again. This time not holding back. Her lips melt into mine like hot butter on a frying pan. Her tongue slips gracefully into my mouth, and I notice how soft she is. Her lips are like two pillows and her tongue is delicate, entangling with mine. It's *different* than kissing a man, than kissing *Finn*. But I like it, *a lot.*

Our tongues dance together, and I accidentally let out a low moan when Gemma's fingers rake through my hair. She kisses me with fierceness but not roughness. She's delicate with me. I want to take in everything in this moment. She tastes like cherries, her tongue extra sweet. I lean my body in closer to hers, the kiss not being enough. My thighs are clenched together as she kisses me. A pool of desire forms in my panties. Well, in my bathing suit bottoms, actually.

"Wow," I say when Gemma eventually pulls back to let us catch our breath.

"I take it you're a fan?"

"Oh, I'm definitely a fan."

"We could kiss some more, if you want."

"I'd like that." I nod.

Gemma lies down with her head on one of the throw pillows, and I lie next to her. The couch is just as comfortable as a bed, if not more. And this way we aren't straining our necks to kiss. Gemma pulls me into her again, this time kissing me softly. She works her way up to kissing me like before. My hands feel the need to touch something, but where do they go when you're making out with a woman?

I settle them on Gemma's hips, and I wonder if I'd like touching her boobs. They're much larger than mine, and I have a feeling she wouldn't mind. Just the thought of touching them makes me think of the last few fantasies I've had about her recently. I moan into her mouth, and she nibbles on my bottom lip. She stops kissing my lips and takes a moment to kiss my neck. I close my eyes and relax into her as her tongue swipes across the nape of my neck. Fuck. Why did that feel so good?

Gemma kisses my neck harder, as if she's about to bite it, and then gently stops. I'm rubbing my thighs together at this point because I'm too horny not to. I take Gemma's hand and guide it to my chest. I need to be touched, and I want her hands on me. Gemma whispers in my ear with hot breath, and I just about combust.

"I think someone likes being with a *woman*."

I know we're supposed to be taking this slow, but something comes over me. I'm absolutely feral for this woman, and that's how I climb on her lap to straddle her. I pull back and look at her quickly, as if to check in and she nods. Giving me all the answers I need. Gemma squeezes my breasts, and through the thin fabric of my dress and bikini top, I feel my nipples harden. I groan into her mouth once again, and I reach for hers. Soft, squishy, and more amazing than I anticipated.

"Fuck. I think I'm close." I don't know what comes over me but between the kissing, all the touching both of us are doing and the grinding— I think I'm about to have an orgasm.

I'm basically riding Gemma's thigh, and she doesn't tell me to stop. If anything, she encourages me and uses her hands to play with my breasts. My nipples feel like fireworks daring to go off in any second. I can feel the orgasm building, and with one last swipe of her tongue across my lips, I'm coming in my panties. I collapse next to Gemma and then cover my face, which has to be as red as my hair.

"I'm so freaking embarrassed," I mutter.

"What? Why?" Gemma pulls my hands away.

"Because I just came in my pants like some teenager." I groan.

"That was fucking hot, first of all. And second, that's totally normal. Your hormones are all over the place right now. I'm sure everything is a little bit more sensitive."

"It is." I nod.

"Exactly. That just made me so turned on."

"Really?"

"Oh, yeah. As soon as we're alone I'll have to do something about it because my panties are probably as ruined as yours." She laughs.

FIFTEEN

Gemma

Norah and I spend the day at Wrenn and Ryleigh's house doing all the things for the wedding that Will isn't doing. Of course, Alana didn't say it like that, but I know that's what it is. She's covering for him even though he isn't doing shit when it comes to this wedding. Sure, it was nice getting to meet everyone else today. I'd heard stories about Alana's friends over the years, but it was nice to put faces to the names. But the wedding was a month and a half away, a lot of this stuff should've been done months ago. Some of the stuff Will had even told Alana he'd done.

Maybe I was just cranky because instead of spending my day off kissing Norah, I had to spend it working on wedding stuff. Not that I wouldn't for Alana, but I didn't like knowing it was because Will had slacked off.

"Are you okay?" I ask Norah.

"Yeah, why?"

"You've just been quiet all day." I frown.

"I'm just tired. I thought that had mostly passed but I think today took a lot out of me." She yawns.

"Why don't you go make some tea? That usually relaxes you."

"That's a good idea." She smiles.

"I'll be right back."

I disappear into my room and head for the bathroom. For some reason my room has a much bigger bathtub, so I thought I'd set up Norah with a bath. I grab a handful of tea lights, candles, and matches from the closet and set them up all around the bathroom. I don't have rose petals or anything like that, but I hope the candles would be enough. I put in some bubble bath to create a lot of bubbles in the warm water. I consider throwing in a bath bomb, but I don't know how she would react to the scents I had. It could make a good thing into a disaster.

"Hey Norah?" I call out when the bath is ready.

"What's—" Norah gasps as she walks into the dark bathroom.

"I thought you'd like a relaxing bath before bed." I smile.

"This is so sweet." Norah's eyes brim with tears.

"I'll leave you be to relax." I kiss her forehead and turn to walk out of the bathroom when she pulls me back.

"What if you stay?" Her green eyes look up at me expectantly.

"You want me to take a bath with you?"

"I mean there's enough room for both of us." Norah shrugs. She's right, the bathtub is huge.

But it isn't that that was holding me back. It is the fact that this would mean we'd be naked in front of each other. So far, all we've done is kiss and dry hump like teenagers. We're taking things slow, and that's okay with me. Sure, I'm using my vibrator a ton more, but I like Norah a lot. I don't want to rush her out of her comfort zone.

"You don't have to," she adds quickly.

"Babe, trust me I want to. I was just making sure you're okay with it. We haven't been naked in front of each other yet."

"I know, but I trust you."

"I do too."

Norah begins to unbuckle the loop on her overall shorts and

lets one strap fall behind her. She pauses and looks at me. I undo the string of my waistband and smirk at her. Norah undoes the other strap, and I kick off a sock. She smiles and lets the overalls fall to the floor. She's wearing a pair of cotton pink panties with a little flower on the front. God, she's freaking killing me. I take off my shirt next and blush as her eyes rake over my chest. Norah slips off her T-shirt and tosses it into the pile of clothes we're making. Her breasts are covered by a thin lace bralette. Her nipples are already hard and poking through the fabric. I bite my cheek and toss aside my pants.

Norah blushes before taking off her bralette and her panties and then gazing at the floor. Fuck, she's beautiful as hell. Her body is sexy, from her full breasts down to her painted toes. If I weren't a nurse and I didn't already know, I probably wouldn't have noticed her darkened nipples or the way her stomach slightly curves for a baby bump. But even with those attributes, she's beautiful.

I toss aside my panties and bra and follow Norah into the tub. She sinks into the warm water and groans lightly. The water covers all the way up to the tops of her breasts, and she smiles at me. I relax into the water and feel her feet near my lap. I reach below the water and take one in my hand. She looks at me quizzically until I begin to massage it for her. I've worked in enough labor and delivery units to know that every pregnant woman loves having their feet rubbed.

"You don't have to do that, you know."

"I know. But I want to." I'm careful not to put too much pressure on her nerves. It might be an old wives' tale that a certain pressure point could put her into early labor, but I'm not about to find out.

"Thank you for this and thank you for being here with me." Norah smiles.

"You're beautiful, do you know that?" I muse aloud.

Norah turns red and pushes a fistful of bubbles at me. They hit my cheek and I blow them away, laughing. I throw back a handful at her and she laughs as they land on her nose. Somehow one thing turns to another and we're having a bubble war in the tub. We're both giggling, and covered in bubbles, Norah sinks into the tub trying to escape getting hit and I reach for her. Instead of getting bubbles, I get a handful of Norah's breast.

Norah looks up at me with wide eyes, and now I'm the one blushing.

"Is this okay?" I ask quietly.

"Yes." She smiles.

I lean in, wipe away the bubbles off her face, and press a kiss to her lips. Kissing Norah is different than the women I've kissed. Sure, it was fun and nice, but kissing Norah feels explosive and exciting. I want to get to know every inch of her body and everything about her. Lately we've spent hours kissing and talking. Going back and forth until our mouths were too tired. Norah falls asleep before I do most nights, and we eventually make our ways to our own beds.

I kiss her lips softly and pull her body toward mine. This is the first time we've been naked together. So I take in every sensation. The way Norah's hips feel under the wet, soapy water. The way she moans under my delicate touch. Her pubic hair tickles my thigh under the water. If I could, I'd bury myself in her body. Norah slides on my lap and straddles me, both of us sitting in the water. I pinch her nipple in my fingers, and she tosses her head back with a throaty moan.

"Wow, that feels so much better than when I do it," she mutters.

"Excuse me? Do you often play with your nipples?" I tilt my head.

"Well, recently yes. I think it's the hormones because I've been...uh...extra horny." She covers her eyes with wet hands.

"God, you're so hot without even trying," I mumble. "Show me what you do."

"W-what?" She looks at me wide eyed.

"Show me how you like your breasts played with, *Norah.*"

Norah leans back so I can see her breasts, and she slides her hand slowly up her stomach and around each breast. Then she takes her nipples in her hands, and tugs on them simultaneously. Norah bites down hard on her bottom lip as she rubs them between her thumb and pointer.

"Fuck it." I swat her hands out of the way and replace them with my own.

Norah moans and then slides off my lap only to pull me on top of her. She plays with my breasts, squeezing them. My breasts are nowhere near as sensitive as hers are. I pull back and sit back in the tub again. This time I pick up her other foot and massage it. Norah looks at me with hooded, darkened eyes. She wants me as much as I want her. But I'm determined to make sure she isn't rushing into anything. I don't want her to worry if this is too soon or question anything about us. So, I pace us. No matter how much I don't want to.

When the bath water eventually turns cold, we get rinse off and get out. Norah heads to her room to put on some pajamas, and I do the same. I blow out all the candles to make sure we don't accidentally set Alana's house on fire. Then I go to look for Norah. When I don't find her in the spare room reading, or in the kitchen snacking, I get a little worried…until I find Norah fast asleep in her bed. Her body is over the covers like she accidentally fell asleep or something. I pull a blanket over her and turn off the lamp next to her bed. I press my lips to her forehead before closing the door behind me on my way back to my room.

Being with Norah is equally simple and complicated. The easy part is being with her; we communicate well, and the chemistry between us is incredible. Sure, she wants things slower than I do, but even that doesn't bother me. She is new to being with women, and the last thing I want is to move too fast and give her a negative experience. What complicates things is the fact that in seven months she'll be having a baby.

I have no idea where that leaves me in the equation. It isn't like her husband is around, and I'll be intruding on something, but am I ready to jump into a relationship that would make me a stepmom before the first anniversary? I love kids, and kids love me. But babies? That's a whole different ballgame. I've done my rotation in obstetrics, and although they're cute and squishy, babies were also terrifying as hell. So many things could go wrong in that first year. Will Norah even have time for a new relationship? I know the baby will have to come first, but am I ready to put my life on hold for that? I don't know.

But the alternative to being with Norah...well, that isn't something I want. I like her, a lot. And I feel connected to her somehow. Maybe Norah will change her mind about me before the baby comes and this won't be an issue anyway. I'm surely getting ahead of myself. We've been seeing each other for two weeks, not two years. Over time, we'll figure out how we fit into each other's lives, won't we?

I completely understand why she did IVF, and I can see the joy emitting from her when she talks about the baby. She was made to be a mom. I just don't know if *I* was. That's what complicates things and also why I don't want to push things to go too fast. I don't want to rush any step of this and lose Norah. Maybe the more I get to know her, the more I'll figure out what I want. I just don't want to hurt her if I decide her having a baby is too much for me. Right now, it's a little bump, a lime that we talked about. But will things be different when the baby comes? Of course it will be.

SIXTEEN

Norah

I'm lounging on the couch shortly after Ryleigh leaves. Gemma is still in the dining room, cleaning up from all the bachelorette party prep. I had a pretty long day at work yesterday, so I feel exhausted. Never mind the fact that I get another bout of morning sickness when Gemma asks about lunch. There is no explanation for the foods that seem to trigger this baby. Sure, sometimes it's actually gross smells and foods, but most of the time, it's completely random. So I lie on the couch, snacking on saltine crackers and reading on my Kindle.

I didn't plan to tell Ryleigh the news about the baby, but now that I have, I feel a little more at ease. The more people who know before the wedding, the easier it is to hide. There will be fewer questions and hopefully not too much attention on my bump. It's still pretty small at this point and easy to hide. But I'll be almost halfway through the pregnancy by then, and I have no idea what size I'll be. At least I think to get my dress in a bigger size. I'll have to cut it pretty close if I need any alterations.

"Are you feeling any better?" Gemma comes over and sits at my feet. She pulls them into her lap and mindlessly begins rubbing them. I feel bad that she's always doing that, but it feels heavenly.

"Yeah." I nod.

"Do you want anything for dinner, or are crackers your dinner?" She laughs, but I know she's not judging.

"Crackers for dinner."

"Gotcha. I'm gonna make a peanut butter and jelly if the smell won't bother you."

"Not at all, but thanks for checking." I smile. Gemma is incredibly considerate when it comes to my oversensitive nose.

"Wanna watch a movie?" She glances at the TV we hardly use.

"Sure. Have any in mind?"

"You know *Twilight* is my comfort movie."

"Let's do it. I haven't seen it since high school," I admit.

"Do not tell me that! That's way too long to go!" Gemma gasps and clutches her chest.

"Okay, then let's watch it." I giggle.

"You're lucky you're cute." Gemma gets up and kisses my lips softly. She disappears into the kitchen to make her sandwich, and I look for the TV remote. I toss my Kindle on the coffee table and get up to find it on the mantle. I stretch out my arms over my head and twist a little. I've been lying on the couch for longer than I care to admit. My body feels a little stiff.

I sit back down with my legs crossed and turn on the TV. I'm not sure what streaming app the movie is on, so I just type it in the search bar. It pops up a second later, and I'm not surprised to see it's on Gemma's previously watched list. It looks like she's halfway through a rewatch. I hit play and pause it on the opening sequence. Then I run to the bathroom to pee because I don't want to miss the movie or get up when I'm comfy again. When I return from the bathroom, Gemma's sitting on the couch.

"Come here." She opens her arms, and I snuggle into her. I rest my head on her chest, and she tugs a blanket over us. It's not really needed for warmth, but more for comfort. Gemma starts the movie, and about five minutes in, I realize how much this movie means to her. She's narrating every line, mumbling them under her breath but still loud enough for me to hear. It's sort of adorable.

When the movie ends, I yawn.

"Bedtime?" Gemma asks.

"Yes," I nod. Part of me wishes I could just stay here and sleep on her. Gemma is comfortable, and I like lying next to her. It has been too long since I slept next to another person. It feels more intimate than sex, in my opinion. But it's a step I'm suddenly ready to take.

"Can I sleep in your bed tonight?" I ask softly.

"Of course." Gemma smiles and squeezes me lightly.

We both stand, I take her hand and she leads me to her bedroom.

"I'm going to brush my teeth and put on my pajamas," Gemma tells me.

"Can we pretend this is a real sleepover and you lend me a shirt to wear for bed?"

"Hell yeah." Gemma nods. She goes to her dresser and pulls out an oversized black T-shirt. When she turns it around, I realize it has Bella and Edward's faces on it.

"This looks vintage," I admire.

"It's mine from when I was in high school. So I guess, it sort of is." She laughs.

"Thanks."

I change out of my clothes and into her shirt while she's in the bathroom. I take off my bra because only psychopaths sleep in bras and leave my panties on. I feel a little shy even though Gemma's seen me naked before. But sleeping next to her half-dressed is new territory for us. I hope my nerves were really hidden excitement.

"Shit, you look way too good in my clothes." Gemma groans. She comes up behind me and palms my ass.

My breath hitches and I lean into her. I smell the fresh scent of spearmint toothpaste and she spins me around to kiss me. Her tongue slides into my mouth and I let her take the lead. I was exhausted but Gemma was lighting a fire inside me. She only kisses me for a moment before pulling away.

"Ready for bed?" She looks at me expectantly.

"Mmm," I nod. Even though bed is the last thing on my mind.

Gemma pulls back the covers on the messy bed, and I get into bed first. She doesn't mention anything about having a particular side, so I stay on my usual side. Gemma slides in next to me and we face each other. She smiles, her dimples showing, and I run my hand over her cheeks. She runs her hand to my chin and pulls me in for a kiss. Her lips linger on mine, and I melt into her body. My body tingles as she kisses me, and my hands go to her chest. She's not wearing a bra either and I groan.

"Before you fall asleep kissing me, we should get some sleep," Gemma says, pulling away.

I want to protest, but before I can, a yawn escapes my lips and we both laugh.

"Okay, fine," I grumble.

"How do you like to sleep?"

"I'm supposed to sleep on my left side I think."

"Yeah, it's better blood flow for you and the baby." Gemma nods.

I turn on my left side and she presses her body behind me, spooning me. I relax as she wraps her arms around me and kisses the back of my head. It's moments like this that make me feel like everything will work itself out. I've been so worried about what might happen once the baby comes and how that will change our growing relationship. Babies were hard on couples who are married for years, how would they be on a brand-new relationship? I know we'll eventually need to talk about it. We talk so openly about everything else, but I think because this scares me, it isn't as easy to bring up. I'm not ready to lose Gemma in this way. So for now, I would see how things progress and hope for the best.

"Oh." A moan slips through my lips and my eyes shoot open. Gemma's looking at me wide eyed and it takes me a second to get my bearings.

"What just happened?" I whisper.

"I think...you were having a, um, sex dream." Gemma clears her throat.

It all comes racing back to me, and my eyes shut tightly as I try to will myself awake. Clearly it was a dream, and I'm not really in Gemma's bed having a sex dream about her. But my eyes are closed, and once again I can see her lips on my breasts and her hands on my pussy, and I open my eyes. Is nothing safe?

"You don't have to be embarrassed," Gemma whispers even though I'm sure my cheeks are burning right now.

"I'm in your bed, and I had a sex dream." I groan.

"It happens to the best of us, and if it helps, it sounded like a good one." Gemma cracks a smile, and I turn my head into the pillow and groan.

"Norah, baby. It's okay. We don't have to talk about it, let's just go back to sleep."

I peek one eye at her. "Well, now I'm sort of awake and horny."

"Oh." Gemma's the one to blush this time. "Would you like me to help you?"

The words send a shiver down my spine, and I nod. I turn over to face her and she brushes my hair back behind my ear.

"Just tell me to stop if I go too far, okay?" She looks at me and I agree.

I want this. She wants this.

Gemma leans in to kiss me, her tongue trailing across my

lips. She tugs gently on my bottom lip with her teeth, and I moan. Her tongue slips in, and she pulls my body into hers. Gemma takes her time kissing me. Nothing about this is rushed despite the fact that I can feel the need growing between us. I palm her breasts through her pajamas, and she tugs at the bottom of my T-shirt. I want to yell at her to take it off and fuck me, but I restrain myself. I want this moment to last between us.

Gemma's mouth starts trailing down my neck. She grabs my breasts in her hands and plays with them gently. They were so sensitive that I let out a greedy moan. Gemma slides up my shirt painfully slow and then dips her head to my chest, taking my nipple in her mouth. She glides her teeth over it, taking the time to suck. My thighs clench together as she switches between each one.

"Please, touch me. More," I finally beg.

"I thought you'd never ask." She smirks and slides her tongue down my stomach.

Gemma stops just above the waistband of my clearly soaked panties. I can smell my arousal from here so God only knows what she's thinking. She presses her thumb to the wet spot on my clit, and my hips buck toward her involuntarily.

"Oh, fuck!" I scream out.

"God, you're so needy." Her eyes are dark with desire.

Gemma tugs my panties to the side and slides a finger down the lips of my pussy. I bite back a moan as I shiver again. Gemma is touching my aching pussy, and I fucking love it. Oh, I am *definitely* into this woman.

"I'm going to fuck you now, okay?" Gemma looks up at me.

"Yes, please," I say with a heavy breath.

Gemma slides down my soaked panties and tosses them aside. I watch as she looks at my pussy with desire. Finn never looked at it like that. We loved having sex; he was great in bed. But when it came to eating pussy, it wasn't his favorite thing. It's not like he wouldn't do it for me, but his heart wasn't really in it, so I usually didn't ask. So, to see Gemma looking at me like her next meal and literally licking her lips? I'm only getting wetter for her.

Gemma presses her tongue to my clit and I almost cum right on the spot. She slides her tongue through my pussy, lapping up all of me, and I can't hold back my moans. I probably sound like something out of a porno, but I don't care. Gemma is taking her time with me, and I'm enjoying every second of it.

SEVENTEEN

Gemma

"Oh, my god! Don't stop!" Norah screams as I make her come.

Her juices drip down my chin as I attempt to clean her pussy with my tongue. I was right about her; she does taste as sweet as those cherries. Her pretty pink pussy pulsates with desire as I witness her orgasm. But the second it is over, I slide two fingers inside her and pump fast. If this is her first time with a woman, I'm going to make it memorable. Which means multiple, mind-blowing orgasms.

"Holy shit!" she screams and clenches her thighs around my head.

Women are fucking amazing, and Norah is no exception. I could eat her out for days. The second I saw her pussy, I knew I was in for a treat. The way she lets go when I touch her goes straight to my ego. Her hair is a mess, red splayed all over the pillows, her body thrashing with each orgasm. And the sounds? Women who are loud are top tier in my mind. Because again, not everyone can do that. Knowing that I'm making Norah scream and curse and come undone? There's nothing else like it.

Norah comes again, and I'm about to go for round three when she pushes my head away gently. I smile and climb up to lay next to her in bed. Her eyes are closed, and she looks like she's sleeping except for the heavy breathing. I slip out of bed to grab a washcloth. I run warm water on it and then wipe it over her pussy. She flinches when I do but relaxes when she realizes what I'm doing. Her pussy is so sensitive right now; I bet one lick would send her to the stars.

"How are you feeling?" I return from the bathroom again, this time with a glass of water for her.

"Mmm, so good," she mutters.

"I brought you some water." Norah sits up next to me and chugs the whole thing. "Do you need more?"

She shakes her head and lies back down.

"You're so beautiful." I smile.

"So are you," she says quietly.

"So, you think you like women?" I laugh.

"I don't know about women in general, but you? Oh, yes. I definitely like you and what you just did." She gushes.

"How do you feel about a midnight snack?"

"Yes, please." Norah smiles and we both jump out of bed.

I turn on the nightlight in the kitchen and look in the fridge for something quick to eat.

"Any suggestions?" I look at Norah.

"Do we have more cherries?" Norah asks and I laugh.

"We do." I grab the container and hand them to her.

"I'm not usually obsessed with cherries, but for some reason I can't seem to get enough." She blushes.

"It's one of the more normal pregnancy cravings I've heard of," I tease.

"What are some of the weird ones?"

"Well, there's the typical peanut butter and pickles. But then I've had women say they craved French fries and milkshakes, ice cream on toast, and toothpaste."

"Just toothpaste? Like straight from the tube?" Norah's face twists in disgust.

"Yeah. I mean it sounds gross to me but." I shrug.

Norah pops a few cherries in her mouth, causing her tongue to turn red. I settle on a bag of Popcorners and chomp away. I steal a cherry from Norah when I'm done and spit out the pit into the garbage. When we're both finished with our snacks, we head back to bed hand in hand. Norah heads to the bathroom while I climb into bed and wait for her. I'm still horny as hell and dying for a release, but I'm not expecting one tonight. Norah is new at this, and I don't want to push her if she isn't ready to reciprocate yet.

"Are you ready to go back to sleep or…" Norah's voice trails as she looks at me. She's standing at the edge of the bed and touches my ankle with her fingers.

"Or?" I raise an eyebrow.

"I thought maybe you could teach me how to…well, get you off?" She blushes and I try not to laugh but she was so fucking adorable.

"Only if you're up for it."

"I think I am." She nods.

"Come here." I reach for her, and she climbs on top of me to straddle my lap. Fuck. She looks like a natural up here.

"What do you like?"

"Well, honestly, I'm not too picky. I have toys and stuff too, but I think we should take it slow with that."

"Yes," she agrees.

Norah leans in to kiss me. Her chest presses into my own, and her hips move lightly on top of mine. I grip her bare thighs and feel her heat through my pajama pants. Her lips press against my neck, and she bites down on my earlobe. I moan audibly into her ear, and she groans back. I love the sounds she makes, it only turns me on more. Norah slides up the sides of my T-shirt and begins playing with my exposed breasts.

First, she takes a moment to look at them, and I mean *really* look at them. They're bigger than hers and are definitely not as perky, but she's eying them with such desire. Then she dips her head between them before taking one in her mouth. She sucks hard on my nipple, and I moan involuntarily. Her other hand is busy pinching and playing with the other nipple, and I move my hips against hers. I reach for her chest, under her shirt, and she momentarily forgets what she's doing. I mirror her movements with my nipples, and she's moaning for me.

"I love how you moan for me." I growl.

"This was supposed to be about you," she grumbles.

I smirk at her attitude. "I can't help that I like pleasing you."

Norah takes my hands and pins them over my head. Her green eyes look darker than normal, and she presses her lips to my ear.

"It's my turn to please *you*," she says in a sultry tone I've never heard before.

Instantly, I'm putty in her hands. She can do whatever she wants to me at this point. I just nod and she goes back to playing with my breasts. Only for a moment because then she asks me to take off my pants. Norah slides off my lap, and I kick off my pants and toss them on the floor. Thankfully, I shaved and wore cute panties to bed, just in case.

"Can I touch you?" she asks looking up at me with big eyes.

"Yes please." I groan.

She giggles and hesitantly touches my pussy over my panties. She's quiet but her breathing changes, and I can tell she's getting turned on. She looks unsure, so I take her hand and guide it to my clit. Norah presses down gently, and I gasp. I tug off my panties to get them out of the way, and she puts her hand back, hovering over my pussy. I guide her again, this time using her two fingers to run up and down my wetness.

"Mmm," I hum lightly.

"You're so *wet*," she gushes.

"That's all you." I smile.

Norah smiles with pride, and I stop guiding her. She takes a second to figure out her next move and then runs her thumb across my clit. When I moan, she touches me again. She uses two fingers and slides them inside me, and I gasp. She has these long and incredible fingers I wasn't expecting to feel so good inside.

"If you curled your fingers right now, you'd probably hit my G-spot," I tell her.

"Like this?" Norah perfectly curls her fingers toward her, and I let out a throaty moan.

"Mmm." I nod.

Norah smiles and leans over to kiss me while keeping her fingers inside me. As she gets more into the kiss, she moves her hand, hitting the same spot over and over. She's a fucking natural. I reach for her breasts as she finger fucks me and tug on her nipples. I am so pent up from the multiple orgasms and all the kissing we've been doing. The taste of the cherries lingers on her lips as she kisses me. I move my hips to get as much friction from her as possible. When she moves her thumb to brush across my clit, I'm gone.

"Oh, I'm coming!" I yell out, tossing my head back into the pillows. I shudder as the orgasm hits me, and Norah doesn't let up until she pulls out her fingers. She looks at her hand, dripping with my wetness and slides them both into her mouth. My jaw drops, and when she opens her eyes, her fingers are clean and her face turns from pleasure to worry.

"What? Should I not have done that?"

"No, no. That was just fucking hot," I admit.

"You taste really good." She blushes.

"Fuck." I pull her in for a kiss. My tongue tangles with hers, and I groan, tasting myself on her lips.

"It's fun, making you come," she says quietly. I love how shy she could be considering she was just finger deep inside me.

"I have no complaints." I smile.

Norah snuggles into my arm, and I pull the covers over us. We're half-dressed but we're both too tired to care. I wrap my arms around her, and she rests her head on my chest. I can smell her shampoo as I take each breath. Norah closes her eyes, so I kiss her forehead and she smiles. She lets out an oversized yawn and then falls asleep within seconds. I wonder if that's a pregnancy thing or a normal thing. The only time I've ever been able to fall asleep that quickly is when I'm drunk.

I watch her as she sleeps, not in a creepy way. Just in a I can't fall asleep that quickly and she's beautiful way. Norah snores lightly and I try to put myself to sleep but I'm not as tired as I thought. I know I'll eventually fall asleep, but it seems like I am about to have a bout of insomnia. It isn't uncommon for me, especially with my weird work schedule. I could probably take some melatonin and be out, but I don't want to.

Norah still isn't my girlfriend, officially. Even though I want her to be. I just don't know how to ask her to be until we have a serious conversation about the future. Where I stand with her and the baby is important to me. And if this is a normal relationship, I'd wait awhile before bringing it up. But because it's anything but normal, I feel like sooner is better than later. I don't want her to be my girlfriend just for a few months later for us to break up because she's a new mom. But I also don't want to be casual with her when I think about how much I like her.

I wish I had someone to talk to about this. Alana and I usually tell each other everything, and it's been hard not telling her about this. But with everything going on with her and Will? I just know this isn't the right time. I don't want her worrying about her wedding and Norah and I possibly not getting along because of our failed relationship. Not that I assume it's going to be a failure, but that *is* a possibility. Plus, I know Norah doesn't want to take any spotlight away from Alana either. So for now, it's something I'll have to deal with on my own—which is probably making it ten times harder. I feel like life is always a little bit easier when you can talk your problems out with a friend.

EIGHTEEN

Norah

"Oh, my gosh!" I shoot up in bed, and Gemma looks at me like I'm nuts. For clarity, it's barely 8 a.m., and we are lying peacefully in my bed until I shout at my phone.

"What happened?" Gemma asks, looking concerned.

"I got the apartment I put an offer on!" I exclaim.

"You put in an offer on an apartment?" Gemma looks surprised.

A few weeks ago, during one of my many pregnancy hormonal spirals, I worried about where the baby and I are going to live. So I started looking online for apartments and stopping by open houses on my way home from work. I know I want to stay in Lovers, so it's just a matter of finding the perfect two-bedroom that is close to work and the schools in town.

"I did. I didn't think I'd get it, so I didn't mention it," I explain.

"Ah." Gemma goes quiet.

"Are you mad?"

"No, not at all. I'm just surprised. You didn't say you were looking for a place, is all." Gemma smiles.

"Well, it's not like I can live here with the baby," I point out.

Gemma nods.

"Do you want to see the place?"

"Of course." Gemma relaxes as I pull up the photos I took when I was there. It's completely empty and has a fresh coat of paint, so it's almost move-in ready. The owners had it ready for a family member who decided to move out of state at the last moment. The living room and kitchen aren't huge, but they're big enough for me and a baby. The bedrooms have beautiful natural light, and the whole place has hardwood floors.

"Do you need help painting?"

"Everywhere has fresh paint, but I do want to paint the nursery before I move in."

"Is that the extra bedroom?"

"Yes. The baby will probably be in a bassinet for the first few weeks in the room with me, but then I want them to have their own room." I smile.

"I think it's lovely," Gemma says with a smile.

Gemma's work alarm goes off, and she gives me a quick kiss on the lips before heading to her room to get ready. We've been taking turns staying in each other's rooms each night, but for the most part, we sleep in the same bed every night. I'm looking at the apartment photos and the confirmation email when I feel a knot in the pit of my stomach. When I move into the new place, I won't be sleeping in the same bed as Gemma anymore.

I don't know what is going to happen with Gemma and me. It's like this invisible thing hanging over our heads that we casually avoid. Gemma is only contracted to work at Lovers General until the end of September. Does that mean our relationship has an expiration date? I don't want to think of it like that, but I don't know what else it might mean. I'm going to be moving and having a baby; is that something Gemma wants to be a part of?

Gemma walks back into the room in her pink scrubs and grabs her phone off the nightstand.

"Do you need anything before I go? I'm just making my lunch," Gemma asks.

"No, I think I'm going to take a shower." I smile. Gemma kisses my lips quickly and disappears into the kitchen.

I kick off the covers, stand up, and notice I feel a little dizzy. I hold my head and grip the side of the bed as I stand. Whoa, that felt like a head rush. I steady my breathing and walk toward the bathroom. I still feel dizzy, so before I turn on the water, I sit on the floor of the bathroom. The room starts spinning, and that's when I know I'm in trouble.

"GEMMA!" I call as loud as I can. It makes my head pound, but I think I hear her coming.

"Norah?" Gemma looks around the room, and I lift one hand to wave to the bathroom. Gemma sees me on the floor and rushes to my side. "What's wrong?"

"I felt dizzy, so I sat down. I don't know what's wrong." I try not to get too upset, but I'm freaking out a little.

"Okay, do you have double vision? A headache?"

"Yeah, I have a headache. Maybe I got out of bed too fast," I explain.

Gemma takes my wrist and checks my pulse, or my heart rate. I honestly don't know which.

"Stay right here; I'll be right back." Gemma runs out of the room and is back minutes later. "Drink this."

She hands me a cup of juice with a straw, and I nod. I sip it, careful not to chug, or else it has a habit of coming back up. I start to feel a little better, and Gemma checks my wrist again.

"I think your sugar went too low. That's more common in pregnancy, and we slept in later than usual. Are you okay?" Gemma brushes my hair out of my face and tucks it behind my ear.

"Yes, I'm sorry. I was afraid I was going to pass out or something."

"No. Don't apologize. You did the right thing; sitting down

and calling for help is the most important thing," she reassures me.

"Thank you. I think I'm okay to stand up." I lean on the counter for support and stand up. I'm no longer dizzy, but Gemma is holding out her arms for me just in case.

"You have an OB appointment today, right?"

"Yeah, in like an hour, actually."

"Okay." Gemma pauses. "Let me drive you."

"What? No. You have work. I'll be fine."

"You were dizzy. What if that happens when you're driving? I can let work know I'll be a little late, and I don't need to come in or anything. I just want to make sure you get there okay," Gemma says.

"Okay." I nod. I have enough anxiety about car accidents that I don't need to risk it. If Gemma is willing to take me, I'll take her up on that.

"I'll sit here while you shower, just in case. Okay?" Gemma looks at me.

"Okay."

I undress and get in the shower. I do feel fine now but it is nice that she cares enough to look after me. When I'm done showering, she watches me get dressed and makes me breakfast. Eggs, toast, and more juice just in case. We get into Gemma's car, and I direct her to the doctor's office. Today is only a checkup for the baby and not a sonogram, so I'm not too worried. They'll check the heartbeat and have me pee in a cup just like they always do.

"I'll be here if you need anything." Gemma smiles as we pull up to the office.

"You won't be bored waiting for me?"

"I've got my Kindle," she says pulling it out of her pocket.

I hesitate before getting out. "You could come up, wait in the waiting room. If you want," I offer.

"Are you sure?"

"Yeah. It's just a checkup, no sonogram today so it's fine," I decide.

"Okay." Gemma puts the car in park and smiles.

Gemma takes my hand, and we walk into the doctor's office. I sign in at the front desk, take the urine cup and head to the bathroom. I leave it at the nurse's station when I'm done and then head back to the waiting room for Gemma. She's scrolling on her phone but puts it away when she sees me.

"You're not dizzy anymore, right?"

"Nope."

"And you'll mention the dizziness?"

"Of course." I smile. It's cute seeing her so protective of me.

"Miss Perry?" the nurse calls out.

I stand up and start walking over. But before I get to her, I stop and look at Gemma. I wave her over ,and she looks surprised but she follows quickly behind me.

"Hello dear, can I have you step on the scale?" The nurse weighs me.

"Anything the doctor should know?" She checks my blood pressure and writes it down on the clipboard.

"I had a dizzy spell this morning, just wanna make sure all's good."

"Okay. Doctor will be right in." She smiles and closes the door behind her.

Gemma's sitting on the empty chair across from me while I sit on the exam table.

"Are you sure this is okay?" She looks nervous.

"You don't have to, but it's okay with me if you're here," I admit. I feel safer with Gemma around, but I don't want her to feel any pressure to stay.

"I'm happy to stay," she reassures me with a smile.

"Hello, Miss Perry. How are we doing today? Oh!" Dr. Greenwald walks in and stops when she sees Gemma.

"Gemma, I work in the ER at Lovers General." Gemma holds

out her hand. Of course, why hadn't I considered that Gemma might know my OB.

"Right, I knew you looked familiar." She smiled. "And this is..."

"I'm just here for moral support today. She had a bit of a dizzy spell, so I drove her in," Gemma adds quickly. Leave it to my OB to ask the questions we haven't even asked ourselves yet.

"Ah, okay so your levels looked good. But let's listen to the heart rate on the doppler just in case, and if there's any irregularities, we can do a sonogram to be safe. But it's quite common for your sugar to dip overnight especially in pregnancy," Dr. Greenwald explains.

I nod and lift up my shirt so she can look at my stomach. It isn't like this is the first time Gemma had seen it, but it feels more intimate. Dr. Greenwald places the doppler on my stomach and we're all quiet while we wait for the heartbeat. A million thoughts run through my head in the seconds it takes her to find the heartbeat.

"Everything sounds good. I'd make sure you keep applesauce, juice, or other snacks by the bed in case you feel dizzy. But if you're friends with a nurse then you're in much better care than most," Dr. Greenwald jokes.

I sigh a breath of relief knowing everything is okay.

"I'll see you back here in a few weeks for the gender and anatomy ultrasound scan." Dr. Greenwald smiles. She heads out the door, and I look at Gemma.

She somehow looks more relieved than I do. It hits me that she's as worried about the baby, and I almost as much as I am. She rearranged her morning just to make sure we're both okay. Not because I had asked her to or even because I wanted her to, but because *she* wanted to. Gemma cares about us more deeply than I originally thought. Maybe Gemma is more invested in whatever this is than I realized.

I've been thinking that we need to have this big conversation about where things are going and how the baby is going to affect that. Part of me always thought it was going to be a negative conversation because this is something Gemma isn't ready for. But maybe I am wrong. It's obviously something we still needed to discuss. But I have a lot more faith in the conversation going positively than I did before.

"You okay?" I stand up and take her hand.

"Yeah, just glad you're both okay." She smiles.

NINETEEN

Norah

Once Gemma drops me off at the house and heads to work, I immediately turn around and head to my car. I stop at the grocery store to buy some fresh flowers and then head to the cemetery. Today is Finn's birthday, and he would've been twenty-nine. I get to his grave, clean out the old flowers, kick off the rocks that have shifted, and sit in front of the stone.

Of course, I begin to cry. I can't help it. It feels safe to cry here.

"I heard the baby's heartbeat today. It's so strong; I wish you could've heard it." I cry. "Not a day goes by that I'm not missing you. This baby is going to know everything about you. I promise."

So much of me wishes Finn was here. I feel angry and sad that I'm going through this alone when I shouldn't have to be. I know it's not right to be angry at him; he wanted to be here. But it hurts so much sometimes to be angry with the universe. I worry about everything that could possibly go wrong with the baby. It seems like there are a million things that could happen, and so many of them I can't even do anything about.

"I know we never talked about it, but I wish I knew if you'd be okay with me moving on. Not in the sense that I'd ever forget you, but maybe letting someone else in too. I've met someone, and they fill me with the same joy you did. I think it has the potential to truly be something. But I'm terrified of making it real. I want to do right by you and the baby. I know they'd love me and the baby, but I'm just scared. I can't lose anyone else."

I'm quiet, like I'm waiting for some kind of response. It feels silly because I know I'm not going to get one. Even if he can hear me somewhere up there, it's not like he has any way to reply. So I sit quietly, just thinking about Finn and life and how I wish he were here.

"Oh, sweetheart, I thought I might find you here today." Mama Perry comes up behind me with a similar bouquet of flowers.

"Hi." I quickly wipe my eyes and stand to give her a hug. She's as warm as apple pie coming out of the oven and just as comforting.

"My knees aren't what they used to be," she says as she sits down next to me.

"I miss him so much."

"I know you do; I do too. Things just aren't the same without him." She pulls me in for a side hug.

"I wonder what things would be like with him here," I say quietly.

"I do too. But I don't think he'd want you sitting around grieving like this."

"What?"

"He'd want you to be happy. I know it. Even if it's with someone else."

"Why do you say that?" Did she hear something I said?

"I just know my son. He loved you more than life. But if he isn't here to make you happy, he'd want someone else to take his place, as long as they are good to you."

For a moment, I think about telling her about Gemma. About our relationship and how she makes me feel, but I just can't. I know I'm looking for a sign, but I can't tell Mama Perry how someone is making me feel the way her son did. It might break her heart.

I think about telling her about the baby too. I'm past twelve weeks now, almost sixteen, according to my app. I'm essentially out of the woods, but I can't. Not yet. I'm too afraid of something going wrong and having to deal with another loss. I don't want to put her through that.

"Why don't you come over for lunch? Jerry is at work, and I don't want to be alone," Mama Perry says about her husband.

"Sure." I nod.

"Were you stopping by your parents' today too?" she asks as we stand.

"Just for a moment." I nod.

"Take your time, dear. I'll be at the house. I'll leave the front door unlocked." She smiles.

"Okay."

Mama Perry squeezes my hand lightly before letting go. I walk toward my parents' grave and give them a quick life update when I know she's out of earshot. It's a quick visit, so I clean their grave and then head for my car. I check my phone and see a few missed texts from Gemma. I text her back, but I don't really feel like texting today. I know I should just say that, but I don't want to make a big deal about today. I'm too overwhelmed with emotions to deal with that right now.

I pull up to Mama Perry's house and suck in a breath. I haven't been here in a few weeks, and it feels different somehow. I know it's all in my head; I'm the one who is different. But I open the front door and announce my arrival.

"In here, dear!" Mama Perry calls back. "I hope you're hungry. I'm making Finn's favorite."

"Mac and cheese?" I guess with a smile.

"Oh, yes. He couldn't go a week without having some. He was miserable in college without it. He begged me to make him some and drive it up." She laughs.

"I remember that. One time he tried to make your recipe, and it came out terrible. We didn't know what we did, but it was not good."

"Well, my secret ingredient is love," she teases.

"He told me when we got married, I'd have to learn from you because he wasn't going to spend his life eating crappy boxed mac and cheese." I laugh, remembering. It was one of the first things he told me after we got engaged.

"Here you are!" She hands me a steaming bowl, and I take in the wonderful smell.

"Mmm," I hum. I'm starving, and this smells delicious.

She sits across from me at the kitchen table, and we both blow on the pasta to cool it off. I take a bite, and I'm in awe. I've been able to make it a few times, but it's never as good as this. Finn always appeased me and told me it was just as good, but I know the truth.

"How's work been?" she fills the silence.

"Good." I smile. "We're having a book signing in the next few weeks from a non-local author. They're visiting, and I convinced them to do a signing."

"That's lovely; I'll have to stop by for that."

The author is Zara Lee, an author from New York who is visiting for the next few weeks. She stopped in the store a few weeks ago, and I started a conversation with her. Then I found out she and Kim are sort of new friends, so I convinced Kim to let me get in contact with her so we could plan a signing. We often have local authors do signings for new books, which is great, but to have someone fresh is exciting.

"Have you looked into moving again, or are you still staying with your friend?"

"I actually just got accepted for a rental in town. I'd love to have you and Papa Perry over when I settle in," I say proudly.

"Of course! Oh! That's so exciting. Let me know if you need anything; I'll grab you whatever I can," she says excitedly.

"I think I have most of what I need in storage, but I'll keep that in mind."

"You've really become a remarkable woman, Norah. I mean, you always have been, but you've been dealt so much at such a young age. Yet you always handle it with such grace. It's incredibly impressive."

My eyes water. "Thank you."

"I mean it. I was worried I'd lose you and Finn when I lost him, so I'm incredibly grateful you stayed present in our lives. I didn't want to lose a daughter as well as a son." She tears up and reaches for my hand.

"Finn and I always wanted to have a close-knit family. Of course, I wish he were here, but I love that you've accepted me and love me as much as he did." I squeeze her hand gently.

When I leave Mama Perry's house, I feel emptier than when I arrived. It's not anything to do with her, but the fact that Finn still isn't here. It's like I expect him to be there waiting for me. I take the long way home and drive past our old house. I think a new family with kids lives in it. I didn't want the details at the time, but now I wish I knew. I park across the street and just look at the house. It's filled with so many memories and so many unfulfilled wishes. Finn and I moved in when we were engaged, and I lived there up until a few months after his death. A little girl runs across the yard, and her dad chases after her. She's wearing a pink tutu and carrying a purple wand, laughing hysterically when her dad finally catches up to her and scoops her into his arms.

I begin to cry; I can't help it. But I'm grateful my windows are up, or else someone might hear me. The dad carries her back toward the backyard, and I close my eyes. I'm only torturing myself being here. I know Finn would be here if he could be. This isn't his fault, but fuck, I miss him so much more than I usually do. I knew I'd be doing this alone, but it's harder than I thought it would be. So much of me wishes Finn were here to experience this pregnancy with me.

It helps having Gemma, but I don't even know how long that will last. I like her, and honestly, that terrifies me. I don't think I can handle another loss right now. My pregnant self is too fragile for something like that. I know Gemma hasn't shown any signs of leaving, but she also hasn't shown any signs of staying either. I'm stupid to think someone who lives a nomadic life wants something so permanent, like a relationship and a baby with someone they barely know.

Before the neighbors recognize me crying on their street, I take off for home. All I want is to lay in my bed and fall asleep. I'm too overwhelmed with the day, and I need a nap. I wipe away my tears as I drive, and I'm careful on each turn. The last thing we need is another car accident on Finn's birthday.

When I get in the house, I fall into my bed and wrap the covers around me. I sob as I think about Finn, pulling one of his old sweatshirts out of the closet. I saved it for days when I feel like this—when it feels like the world is crumbling and I need stability. He used to be my rock, and even now, I cling to his sweatshirt and inhale deeply. I can still smell him on it; somehow, after all this time, it still smells like him, and I try to calm myself down.

Slow breaths with each inhale. I close my eyes, and it's like he's next to me.

More breaths, and I open my eyes. The scent of Gemma is still on my pillow. Somehow, that relaxes me just the same. My heart races, and I struggle to calm it down. She's mandarin shampoo and lilac perfume. I touch her side of the bed and wish she were here with me. Somehow, I know she'd know exactly what to say right now.

TWENTY

Gemma

I've been texting Norah most of the day, but for some reason she isn't replying like normal. She replied a bit, but only in short one word answers like she was mad or something. I tried not to read into it and decided to give her some space. Maybe she is upset or emotional after getting dizzy this morning. I know it can be scary for some people to experience a dizzy spell like that. Especially, while pregnant. I keep checking my phone to see if she's come out of her mood, but her silence is my answer.

"You okay?" Elodie asks. She was keeping an eye on a laboring mom. There was no room in the labor unit, and she wasn't far enough along to bring her to a room. So she was hanging out in the ER until the labor progressed.

"Yeah, my… I don't know what she is technically, but she's acting weird today." I frown.

"You're going to have to explain that one to me." She laughs.

So, I start at the beginning since we have nothing but time. I tell her about Norah and I and how we are taking things slow but she's also pregnant and grieving. I run her through the timeline leading up until today, and how she's acting weird.

"Okay, I think you're right. She's probably just spooked

about the baby. Dizzy spells are scary and so is pregnancy, so when you put them together you get multitudes of scary," Elodie says.

"I don't wanna bother her; it just isn't like her."

"Maybe give her some space and then when you get home make her dinner or bring her home her favorite snack. Something that shows you care but you aren't in her face."

"That's a great idea. She's been devouring cherries these days. I'll stop at the market on the way home and grab her some fresh ones and flowers."

"That's perfect." She smiles.

Ryleigh's texting me about the bachelorette party and asks how Norah is. I think it's sweet that her friends are checking in on her, but I sort of like that they check in through me sometimes too. It isn't a roommate thing, it is a sort of girlfriend thing.

> RYLEIGH:
> I was thinking we should plan something for Norah.

> ME:
> Like what?

> RYLEIGH:
> Like a baby gender reveal party. I think they're sexist but Norah's always wanted one.

> ME:
> Do you think she'd want to now? She still hasn't told everyone yet.

> RYLEIGH:
> Let me handle that. Can we have it at your place?

> ME:
> Of course!

Maybe a gender reveal was a good idea. As long as we didn't

burn down the house in a big reveal or something. Norah loves all the baby stuff that came with being pregnant so why wouldn't she want this? We could have it after the wedding if she's worried about telling her friends or something. Ryleigh knows everyone else better than I do, so I'm sure she'll know what's best.

After work I stop by Lovers Market and grab a fresh bouquet of roses, a bag of cherries, and some electrolytes for Norah. I figure it can't hurt to drink a little in the morning before getting up, just in case she feels dizzy again. When I step into the house, something feels off. It's eerily quiet and I can't put my finger on it, but it feels like something is wrong. So I put the stuff down in the kitchen and look for Norah.

"Norah?" I call her name, but she doesn't respond.

I find her in her room, curled up in a ball on her bed.

"Norah? Are you okay?"

"I'm fine," she mumbles quietly.

"Do you wanna talk?" I step toward her hesitantly. Something's definitely up.

Norah's silent.

"I can give you some space if you need to be alone. I don't wanna overstep, but if you want to talk, I'm here too."

Norah doesn't say anything.

"I'll go change out of my scrubs. Give me two minutes."

Norah's silent so I quickly head to my room and grab a change of clothes. I grab a fresh pair of pajamas and head back to Norah's room. It is only six p.m. so I am shocked to find her in bed already, but I guess that's what she needs. When I get back to her room, she's turned over and I can tell her face is red and puffy from crying. I stand at the edge of the bed, and she moves over enough to let me in but still doesn't talk.

"Are you sure you don't wanna talk? It might make whatever's up feel better."

"How can I talk to someone who might not be here soon," she snaps.

"What?" I raise my head off the pillow, and she hops out of bed.

"You're leaving at the end of September, aren't you?" she says angrily.

"I mean, that's when my contract with the hospital is up—"

"Exactly! So why should I open up to you when you're going to be gone in another month?"

"Norah, where is this coming from?" I reach for her, but she juts her arm back like she's been shocked.

"It's the truth! You're leaving. We're taking this slow, but this isn't even anything because it has an expiration date and we both know it."

"It doesn't have to be that way," I say quietly.

"Are you kidding me? How else could it be?" I've never seen this side of her. I can't tell if this is a hormonal outrage or an actual fight. Either way I'm doing my best to stay calm.

"Norah, why don't we just talk about this?"

"No. What's there to talk about? You're going to leave. So why are we going through the motions?"

"Do you mean with us?"

"Yeah." Her jaw clicks.

"I thought there was something here. I thought we were trying to see what might be between us," I say quietly.

"And then what? You leave and I'm alone, except I'm not alone because, oh yeah, I have a baby coming in a few months."

"Is that what this is about? It's perfectly normal to have worries about having a baby. But you aren't going to be alone."

"No! It's not about the baby! It's about us. And how this is probably the worst time for us to be starting something or seeing each other or whatever you want to call it," she snaps.

"I just don't know where all of this is coming from." I sigh.

"It's coming from me! From logic because I haven't been thinking clearly and I don't want to do this anymore. In fact, I'm done with this conversation, and I'm done with this." She holds open the bedroom door and waits for me to leave.

"I'm not leaving."

"What?" She looks surprised.

"You can have your big feelings and you can get upset, but I'm not going anywhere. I'm serious when I say I'm not leaving. So yell all you want, but I'm here."

"I don't want to do this anymore."

"I don't think that's how you really feel." I'm not trying to antagonize her, but I really don't think this is about us. She wouldn't throw a fit like this when I haven't even done anything. This is about something bigger than us.

"I want you to go."

"I'm going to respect your choice and give you some time to cool off, but I'm not going anywhere."

I walk out the door, and Norah makes a point of locking it behind me. I head to the kitchen and put the cherries in the fridge, the flowers in a vase with water, and then make a quick sandwich. I grab my Kindle, a blanket, and my pillow and sit outside Norah's door. I decide to give her some time and then I'll knock and see if she's ready to talk yet. I eat my sandwich quietly while I read and then look at the clock. I stand up and knock on the door.

"Go away!" Norah yells. But this time it sounds like she's crying.

"Are you crying?"

"No!" Norah yells but I can still hear her quiet sobs.

I sink down against the door and sigh. I wish I could knock down the door and tell her it will all be okay. I don't know what is going on but one thing was clear: she needs me to show her I'm not going anywhere. So I decide to spend the night in front of her door.

"I'm not going anywhere, Norah. I promise," I tell her through the door.

She doesn't reply but she's still crying. I press my hand to the door, and I wish like hell I could be doing more. I feel so helpless right now, but I can only imagine how Norah's feeling. I try to stay awake for as long as possible, but I just worked a twelve-hour shift and I'm exhausted. When I finally hear Norah's cries turn into snores, I decide it's okay to sleep. I prop my pillow against the wall and lie down in front of her door. It's not like she's going anywhere tonight, and the bathroom is in her room.

It's one of the first nights that I'm not sleeping next to Norah, and I hate it. I feel so alone and empty without her snores in my ears and her body on my chest. It's become more and more clear to me today that I'm not ready to live without her. I've been putting off having "the talk" with her for weeks now, and now it seems so stupid. I'm not going anywhere, and of course I'm staying here. If Norah picked up and said tomorrow she wanted to move to the moon, I'd follow her in a heartbeat. She is someone I'm falling for, and I'm not about to let her go. After seeing her on the bathroom floor today and thinking the absolute worst about the baby, I'm not ready to let that go either. I thought when she was on the ground that I was finding her in the middle of a miscarriage and my heart sank. I know how much she loves that baby and truthfully, I've come to love it too.

Norah and the baby are a package deal that I'm ready for. Maybe at first I was a little bit scared, but now I can only imagine having both of them in my life. Norah and I have taken this slow but truthfully, she'd been wrapped around my fingers since the day I met her. As soon as I laid eyes on her, it was like I needed to know her. I wasn't looking for someone like her or even to be in a family, but the more I think about it, the more I know they are my family.

When Norah wakes up tomorrow, I'll finally tell her how I feel. I'll lay it all on the line, and if she still wants to let this go, then fine. But I need her to know how I feel and that I'm not going anywhere. I care deeply for her, and I want her to be happy, even if that isn't with me. I'm going to give her the chance to see that having me is an option. That I can get a job here and we can live together or keep taking things slow, but I'll be here for whatever she needs. I can't imagine my life without her anymore, and I'm not going to.

I fall asleep in the most uncomfortable position possible, and I sleep like absolute shit. But I promise myself it's worth it because I'm not going to risk losing Norah. She needs to see how committed I am to her and that I'm not going anywhere. Physically or emotionally.

TWENTY-ONE

Norah

My eyes hurt, you know when they sting and burn from crying so much? I'm sure if I look in the mirror, they'll be puffy and red too. I don't know how long I was crying for because at some point I fell asleep. That's how upset I was; I cried myself to sleep. I picked a stupid fight with Gemma, and I was too proud to admit it. Now I probably pushed her away with my words and she's gone. I get out of bed, ignoring the mirror on my way to pee. But when I wash my hands and catch a glance, I'm glad there's no one here to see me. I look like crap. My stomach growls, and I groan.

I open my bedroom door to get some breakfast, and I scream when I see a lump outside my door.

"Why are you screaming?" Gemma mumbles with a yawn.

"What the hell are you doing out here?" I clutch my chest.

"Sleeping."

"But why?"

"I told you I wasn't going anywhere." She shrugs as if it's obvious.

The tears start pouring down my cheeks before I can stop them. Gemma jumps up and looks at me with wide eyes.

"What's wrong?"

"I—I'm so sorry!" I cry and she pulls me into her chest. I sob into her T-shirt, and I don't stop.

"It's okay." She rubs my back gently and I inhale her scent. She's all warmth and lilac perfume.

"Yesterday was Finn's birthday," I say quietly.

"Okay. Thank you for telling me that," she says.

"I went to visit his gravestone at the cemetery and ran into his mom," I add.

"How was that?"

"I miss him so much." I cry.

"Of course you do." She nods. "You love him and he's gone, of course you miss him."

"I-it doesn't bother you that I miss him?" I pull back to look at her.

"Of course not."

I don't say anything, just looking at her.

"Norah, you were *married* to him. You had an entire life with him, and he *died*. He's not some ex you're not over; you're always going to love him. And now you're carrying his baby. That's another added layer to grieve. I can only imagine what you're going through." Gemma looks at me softly.

"It just hurts sometimes."

"Promise me something?" Gemma tips my chin back.

"What?"

"Instead of pushing me away, next time you're scared or missing him, you talk to me about it. I know I don't feel the same way you do. But I can listen and try to be there for you as much as I can be."

"Okay." I nod. That was fair. "I-I was scared you didn't want to deal with me and the baby and all my baggage."

"Norah, I like you. I mean, I really like you. You, the baby, your grief, none of it scares me. I just didn't want to push and overstep. This is your first sapphic relationship and your first relationship after you lost someone you love. I want to be respectful of that, but I'm sorry if that came across as me not wanting you."

"I really like you too." I wipe my eyes. Gemma's still holding my chin, and she leans in to softly kiss me.

"Will you be my girlfriend? We can still take things as slow as you need, but I'd love to know you're mine," Gemma says.

"I'd like that." I smile. I don't feel pressured to say yes or worry, if anything I feel an ease about being Gemma's.

"Can we go sit on the bed or on a couch? My back is killing me." Gemma groans with a wince.

"I'm sorry." I frown.

"It's okay, I'd do it again. I told you I wasn't going anywhere." She smiles.

I lead her in my bedroom, and we lay in my bed. She wraps her arms around me, and I relax into her chest.

"Why don't you tell me about him? If you want to."

"Really?" My eyes light up.

"He's someone you loved, and he's the baby's father. I'd love to know more about him. If that's okay."

"I didn't want to talk about him too much, I didn't know if it would be weird," I admit.

"I assume you're going to tell the baby about him, right?" I nod. "Then it would be weird if I didn't know about him."

"He was incredibly funny, and kind. He always knew how to make me laugh no matter what kind of a day I was having. And he knew me like the back of his hand. I wouldn't have to say anything, but he'd just know. He had this ease about him that I haven't felt with anyone else but…" I stop myself.

"But what?"

"Well, I haven't felt this ease with anyone else, but you," I admit.

"Yeah?" She smiles.

"I just feel safe with you. Since the day I met you, it felt different."

"I feel the same way."

"Really?"

"Oh yeah, I thought I never had a shot though."

"I didn't know I even felt that way but then I met you."

"I want to be as involved as you want me to be with the baby," she says quietly.

"What does that mean?"

"Well, if you want me to keep a distance at first because this is so new, I can. Or I can be there for feedings and diaper changes and everything else."

"I want you involved in the baby's life, but I need to take that part slowly."

"I understand that. I just don't want to be shut out before we even have a chance to see where this goes."

"Okay." I smile.

All this time I was worried about Gemma not wanting me or the baby or us, but I was wrong. She was in this probably more than I was. Sure, this terrifies me but I'm relieved to know how she feels about me.

I lean in to kiss her lips, taking the time to swipe my tongue across hers. Our tongues battle for a moment until she gives up control. Her arms pull me tightly against her, and I run my fingers through her hair. I moan into her mouth, and she reaches for my ass. I tug on the bottom of her T-shirt, and she pulls back suddenly.

"Before we start this, I haven't showered, and I worked all day yesterday…"

"I don't care." I shrug.

"Really?" Gemma raises an eyebrow.

"I really. Don't. Care." Between each word, I place a wet kiss on her neck.

"Mmm, okay." Gemma nods and tosses her shirt over her head and off the bed.

I climb on Gemma's lap to straddle her and take each breast in my hands. God, they were so fucking big. They didn't fit in my hands at all, but I loved playing with them. I dip my head to the left and take her hardened nipple in my mouth. I suck on it until she groans out in pleasure. They definitely aren't as sensitive as mine but that makes it all the more fun to play with. I take turns playing with her nipples and kiss all over her full stomach and chest. She's a bigger woman, but she's confident in her body; it's something that draws me to her. She doesn't shy away from her body or the stretch marks it has. Which only makes me feel better about the ones mine is making.

"I think I want to try something." I bite my bottom lip.

"Okay?" Gemma looks at me curiously.

"Would it be okay, if I ate you out?" I blush asking.

"Fuck please. You never have to ask that."

"Well, you might have to guide me. I'm not sure how good I'll be." I'm nervous to say the least. This is a whole new territory. But it's something I wanted to explore with Gemma.

"No pressure." Gemma presses a kiss to my forehead, and I relax a bit.

I slide off Gemma's lap so she can take off her pants and underwear, which is a pair of black cotton panties. Her pussy looks similar to mine, nothing scary about it. Not necessarily hot either, but then again it wasn't like I love the way dicks look. I slip between her legs and begin lightly kissing her thighs. Gemma's legs open involuntarily, and I notice how wet she is. Her juices cover her pink folds.

I decide to test the waters with my hands first. I run my two fingers across her clit and down her slit, getting them nice and wet. Gemma writhes as I touch her, and I realize I'm probably teasing her more than I intend to. I bring my fingers to my lips and lick her off me. She's sweeter than I anticipated. I'm used to Finn, who, despite his best efforts, did not taste the best.

With that in mind, I return to between her thighs and press my face to her pussy. Gemma's breath hitches as I make contact with her clit. I suck on it lightly, lighter than I did her nipples, and then swirl my tongue down her pussy. She reaches for my head and grips my hair tightly as I press my tongue to her clit again. I try to think of the things she did to me and listen to her body. Everything I need to know about how to make her come is in the way she reacts.

"Mm, yes! Suck right there," Gemma encourages me when I return to sucking on her clit.

I drag my finger up her pussy and easily slide it inside her. She gasps, and I know she's enjoying what I'm doing. I smile to myself. Maybe this isn't as complicated as I thought it would be.

"C-can you add another finger?" Gemma moans.

I nod, looking up at her, but between her belly rolls and her holding my hair, I can't see very much in front of me. I remove my finger and add a second one, slowly teasing her insides. I don't know what I'm looking for but if I find her G-spot, she'll definitely let me know. I curl my fingers gently like she has done to me. But when she doesn't make any new sounds, I know I haven't found it. I want to keep going, keep tasting her, but my jaw is killing me. I pat on her thigh, and she lets go of my hair, letting me come up for a breath.

"I'm sorry, I needed a breather," I admit.

"Please don't apologize, that was amazing for a first timer." She smiles. Gemma reaches on the nightstand for my cup of water and hands it to me.

"You made it look easy with me, but shit, that's some work." I laugh.

"It takes some practice, and breathing through your nose can help."

"I was fine breathing, but my jaw got tired."

"Yeah. We might have to build up your endurance." She winks.

"I might be okay with that."

I hand her back the glass of water, now empty, and relax in her arms.

"So, what's the plan with you moving out?" she asks quietly.

I hesitate. I hadn't really thought much about it between yesterday and today. But deep down, I know my answer.

"I'm still moving out. I want to be settled and have my own space for the baby and I before they arrive."

"And that's definitely going to be here in town?"

"Yes. I got a place about ten minutes from here."

"Okay." She nods. "I'll talk to my boss first thing tomorrow about any permanent positions at the hospital, and then I'll start looking for somewhere to live."

"Are you sure?"

"I'm sure that I want to give us time to explore this. And we can't do that if I'm moving to another state. You can't have a newborn and be in a long-distance relationship; it would be too much."

"But you don't mind giving up traveling? Don't you enjoy that?"

"I don't mind staying. I *want* to stay. I do enjoy traveling, and you're right, I've never given it up before. But it's because I've never had a reason to."

And just like that, Gemma's making me cry all over again.

TWENTY-TWO

Gemma

It's only been a week since Norah became my girlfriend, but with all that's happened, you'd think it has been longer. The day after we became girlfriends, I put in an application with my boss for a permanent ER nurse position. She's fairly certain I'm going to get it and applying is just a formality. They've been trying to hire someone more permanent for the last few years now. That led to me making sure it was okay with Alana that I stayed in the estate house until I found somewhere to live. She almost jumped for literal joy when I told her. I think she was happy we'll be in the same town for a little longer.

This also led to me telling her about Norah and I. I told Norah I needed someone to talk to about this, and I hated lying to Alana. She understood right away, and Alana was shocked but overjoyed at us getting together. Her jaw dropped and she thought I was joking at first, but she eventually picked her jaw up and hugged me again.

Norah's attempting to pick up a can of paint, and I race to her side to grab it from her.

"I'm able to pick things up you know. Dr. Greenwald said I can lift up to twenty pounds right now," Norah says stubbornly.

"Yes, but you don't need to lift anything when I'm here," I insist.

"Fine." Norah rolls her eyes but follows me into her apartment.

We spent the last two days deep cleaning the place. Mostly me with the deep chemicals and then when that was aired out, Norah came in with the touch up stuff. I didn't mind helping out, and there was no way I was letting her breathe in any toxic fumes. Now I'm carrying in the paint for the nursery. She'd decided on a gender-neutral gray for the walls and was going to accent the decorations with a color when she picked out a theme. Personally, I like the giraffe theme she had saved, but she's still torn.

"It would be so much easier if we knew what I was having." She makes a face.

"Take that up with Ryleigh." I put my hands in the air in defense.

"I know you helped her plan the whole thing." She stares me down, and I laugh.

I couldn't lie to Norah if I tried, which is how she got it out of me that Ryleigh wanted to plan a gender reveal party. Norah ended up telling the rest of her friends about the baby and then gave Ryleigh the go ahead for the party. I was pretty sure Ryleigh and Alana were taking over the gender reveal but I was in charge of getting them the actual gender envelope.

Norah had invited me to the ultrasound with her. I've seen plenty of ultrasounds at work, and I've even done a few in rotations, but nothing prepares you to see your own kid on the screen. Norah was all laid out with the gel on her growing belly. It's a baby bump if you ask me, but she's starting to show, and it's sort of the cutest thing. Norah held my hand the whole time, and I watched as the baby moved all over the screen. It was certainly active, even though Norah hadn't felt any movements yet that was normal. With babies, everyone is different. But hearing the baby's heartbeat and seeing it on the screen with

To Be Loved

Norah's hand in mine. Wow. It's surreal to say the least. I didn't expect things to go this way but now that they have, I can't imagine them any other way.

So I got the envelope from the doctor, and the only one who knows the gender is Ryleigh. She is planning some cute reveal that she promised wouldn't end up on a YouTube fail video. She's having us all dress up with whatever color we think the baby might be. But that's all Norah knows; we won't tell her when the party is, and she made us promise to keep it small.

"Why don't I start painting the baby's room and you relax on the couch? You've been on your feet all day."

"Fine, but only because my feet hurt in these shoes." Her ankles are starting to get a little swollen, and I want her to be careful. She puts her feet up on the coffee table, and I relax a little.

Apparently, she has a lot of furniture in storage from when she owned a house with Finn. It makes sense that she didn't get rid of everything. I mean, she knew she'd eventually need it. She hired movers to bring it out of storage, and while the baby's room is empty, the rest of the apartment has a lot of her stuff. She isn't moving in officially until after the wedding, but at least she feels a little more settled. I know she is worried about not having time when she gets more pregnant.

I disappear into the baby's room, open all the windows, and open the paint. I'm in an old pair of scrubs that have some stains I can't get out. The paint is safe for pregnant people to smell, but I don't want to take any chances, so I closed the door too. I fill the tray with paint and start on the full wall. Norah spent three hours picking out this color today, so I'm positive she likes it. She must be watching TikTok videos on her phone or something because I hear her laugh every so often.

"GEMMA!" Norah screams my name from the other room. I drop the paintbrush in the paint and rush to her side.

Norah's standing in the middle of the living room, looking down at her stomach through her overalls. Instantly I feel an overwhelming sense of dread. I'm an ER nurse, I know all the things that could be going wrong right now. I have flashbacks to that day I found her sitting on the bathroom floor. I'm terrified to ask, but then I see Norah's smile.

"The baby's kicking!" She grabs my hand, not caring that it's covered in paint, and drags it to her bump.

We're both quiet for a second, and then I feel a small but defined movement under my hand. I gasp and look at Norah smiling. Not just smiling, but her entire face is lit up. Ear to ear smile and a twinkle in her eyes.

"Holy crap," I mumble.

"I was just standing out here, looking around to see where I could hang this picture frame, and then the baby kicked!" she explains.

"That's so amazing." I smile. My cheeks hurt from how much I've been smiling lately. But I guess that's what love does to a person.

"Wait, they might do it again," she says proudly.

Sure enough, seconds later there's another light thump through her overalls, and I'm in awe. I let go of her belly and realize I've left behind a handprint.

"Oh, crap," I mutter. "I'm sorry."

"No, it's sort of sweet. Now we have a memento from this moment." Norah smiles, and I can't breathe for a moment.

She's so freaking beautiful, and in this moment I'm in absolute awe of her. If you ask her, she'd think that because her hair is a mess or that she's not wearing makeup, she's plain. But to me, I only see the real her in these moments. She's looking at her belly, and I'm watching how much she loves this baby. I'm falling for her harder than I ever expected.

"I'm so glad I'm here for this."

"I am too." She smiles at me softly.

"Why don't I finish painting the first wall and we go out to eat? We can go wherever you want."

"Okay!" Norah says excitedly.

I kiss her forehead lightly and then retreat into the nursery. I finish up the wall I'm painting and clean up the brushes for when I come back. I close the windows and find Norah laying on the couch looking at her phone. She looks exhausted and I wonder if she's going to have any energy to go out to eat tonight.

"Do you think—"

I cut her off. "Of course."

"You didn't even hear what I was going to ask." She frowns.

"You want to know if we could order takeout and bring it back to the house instead of going out." I sit down and take her swollen feet in my hands. She groans as I start to rub them for her.

"How'd you know?"

"Because you've had a long day. There's no reason why we should get all dressed up and go out when we can do the same thing at home but undressed." I wiggle an eyebrow.

"Oh. I like that plan." She blushes a deep red.

"I thought you might."

Norah is hornier than a teenage boy, which means most days —and nights—we end up having sex somewhere in the house. The other night I caught her using one of the vibrators in the shower on her clit. Of course, I promptly joined her and made her come three more times.

"What are you thinking about?" She pokes a toe at me.

"The other night when I made you come four times in a row." I smirk.

"Technically, one of those times I got you started."

"My bad, I guess I'll have to make up for that tonight then."

"Mmm." Her stomach growls and we both laugh.

"But food first," I say, and she nods.

She swings her feet off my lap, and I pick up her shoes. I put one on each foot and then help her off the couch. She doesn't really need help, but I love any excuse to hold her hand. We close up her apartment and then head for town. Norah calls into Teddy's for an order and I go in to grab it. Luckily, Wrenn's working so when it isn't ready yet, I have a moment to chat with her.

"Look who it is." Wrenn smiles. "What can I get ya?"

"Actually, I'm just waiting for some food, but I thought I'd come say hi." I smile.

"I hear you and Ryleigh are planning a stripper for my sister? I think that's hilarious."

"It's not a bachelorette party without one." I shrug. It isn't like seeing a naked man does anything for me, but it'll be a funny story at least.

"She's going to flip." Wrenn chuckles.

"She'll get over it."

"Where's your girl? Or is that who the food is for?"

"Yeah, she's in the car. We spent the day painting her new place, so we're headed home to relax," I explain.

"Got it. I'll be sure to add some extra fries for mama then," Wrenn adds with a wink.

"Much appreciated." I laugh.

Wrenn disappears to tell the kitchen to add more fries and comes back holding my large bag of food. I have no idea what Norah ordered, but I don't care. I hand Wrenn my credit card and add a hefty tip on top. I worked in a bar during college, and I lived off tips for a while. I know Wrenn is looking to move out of town eventually, so I'll help anyway I can. She smiles when she sees what I've done, and I head out with the food.

Norah's waiting in the car, her phone connected to the speakers playing TikTok videos. I swear that girl lives on that app. She smiles when she sees me, and I swear I lose all the air in my lungs. I feel like I'm a lovestruck teenager around her sometimes. She just had this effect on me that no one else ever has. So when I get in the car, I pull her in for a kiss.

TWENTY-THREE

Gemma

"How does something like this even work?" Norah eyeballs the box of toys on the bed.

"Which one?"

"The strap on…like I get the mechanics, but the putting it on looks complicated." She tilts her head.

"It's not. It's just like putting on panties and then you have a fake dick." I laugh.

"Is that something you like to do or something you like done to you?"

"Mostly doing. Once in a while I don't mind if someone takes charge."

"Hmm."

"Norah baby, you know all you have to do is ask if you want me to fuck you with the strap."

"I know. I think I'd like you to." She blushes.

"Get naked for me and lay on the bed, baby."

Norah does as I tell her, taking off all her clothes and laying naked on the bed. I get undressed just as quickly and put on the strap. Norah watches me carefully and dips a hand between her thighs. As she spreads her legs for me, I can see her pretty pink pussy dripping with desire. I loved how ready she was for me.

She circles her clit with her fingers and then drags them through her folds.

"Fuck. I might just want to watch you do that all night." I groan.

"I thought you were going to fuck me." Norah bats her eyelashes at me. She knows what she does to me, how she has this effect on me.

"Mmm, yes, baby." I push her hand away from her pussy and slide my fingers up her folds. I slide them back down and push two fingers inside her. Her hips raise off the bed and she gasps as I pump them hard and fast. Just as quickly, I remove them and use her wetness to coat the end of the strap.

"Fuck." She moans.

"It might be a little big, so just let me know if you need me to stop." I tell her. She nods and I climb on the bed to position myself between her legs.

I slide the tip of the strap down her pussy and start to ease inside of her. Norah keeps eye contact with me, somehow making it even hotter as I slide inside her. She spreads her legs open wider and I lean forward to fill her completely. Then she props her leg on my shoulder and my eyes almost pop out of my head.

"How fucking flexible are you?" I groan.

"I might've done a lot of yoga in my life." She smiles.

I grip her thigh and kiss her ankle, holding her as I start to move my hips. Following the sounds of her pleasure, I rock back and forth. Norah relaxes into the pillows, her red hair a mess behind her. I used my free hand to reach between us and stroke her clit.

"Oh!" she cries as I make contact.

"How do you feel, Norah baby?" I smile.

"S-so fucking good." She stutters.

I thrust my hips further into her, diving deep into the bed. My thumb stays on her clit, stroking small circles in her wetness. I could hear the sounds of the strap sliding in and out of her. It was like when you mixed fresh Mac n cheese in a pot. Wet and delicious.

Norah reaches for my breasts and starts playing with one of my nipples. I circle her clit even faster and move my hips at a slower pace, just to throw her off. She gasps and I watch as I pick up the pace and her breasts begin shaking with each thrust. They were never small, but lately her boobs had gotten a bit bigger and I definitely was not complaining. Full and sensitive, they were way too much fun to play with. One time, I was able to make her cum without even touching her pussy.

"Gemma! I'm gonna cum!" she cries loudly and I love the sounds of her orgasms.

"Come for me, Norah baby." I tell her and move my hips even faster.

Norah cries out my name and grips my arm as she cums for me. I feel her juices soaking my thighs and her leg falls from my shoulder back down to the bed. Her head falls into an array of pillows and I pull out of her slowly. The strap is covered in Norah's juices and I fight the urge to lick it clean. Instead, dipping my head down between her thighs and taking a fresh lick. Norah's legs immediately clench my head tightly and I smile.

"I'm s-so sensitive." She mutters.

"Want me to stop?" I look up at her.

"N-no." She moans.

So I lick Norah's pussy, tasting how sweet she is. Which makes sense for how much fruit this woman eats. I swirl my tongue around her clit and then suck lightly. Her hips go flying into my face and I have to hold them down. I reach up to play with her nipples and that's where I lose her. My fingers twist and pull on them. My tongue sucks on her clit and she's panting all over again. Norah cums once again, but this time all over my face.

"Gemma! S-stop please." She groans and I happily move my

face away from her pussy. I move my hands off her breasts and lie on the pillow next to her.

"Mmm, too much, baby?" I kiss her cheek. She's still panting away like she just ran a marathon and hasn't even opened her eyes yet.

"No, but fuck, I liked you being all sexy and powerful like that. You're hot with the strap on." She praises.

"Oh, yeah?"

"Definitely. Whenever I can feel my legs, we should do that again."

"Here, drink some water." I grab her cup from the nightstand and hand it to her.

Norah sits up and sips it slowly. We both don't want her getting dizzy from too many orgasms. That might not be so much fun to explain to the doctor. She hands me an empty glass and then settles on my chest to relax. I wrap my arms around her and kiss the top of her head. Then I look down and start giggling. I don't mean to, but the strap on is just hanging around, swaying in the air.

"What's so funny?" Norah looks up at me but then down at my waist and starts laughing too.

"I just didn't expect to see it like that." I laugh.

"Do you need to take it off? Is it like uncomfortable?"

"Nah, I mean definitely before we fall asleep. But I'm okay for now."

"I might fall asleep." Norah admits.

"That's okay. You probably need your rest. You're growing a whole other person."

"Yeah, this shit is exhausting." She laughs.

"Do you want a snack or anything before bed? Did you take your prenatal?" I know she usually takes it in the morning, but sometimes she forgets and takes it before bed.

"I'm okay and yes, I took it with breakfast today." She smiles.

Norah pulls the sheet over her naked body and I yawn. I didn't think I was tired, but somehow whenever I was in bed with her, I'd start to feel the day creeping up on me. Norah was tracing small circles over my chest and I reach to lay a hand on her belly. I didn't usually touch it, not that I'd go out of my way to not, but I just never really did before. So this time I place my hand on her stomach and she tenses.

"Sorry, should I not?" I pull back, but she stops me.

"No, I liked it. But your hand was cold." She explains.

"Whoops." I relax my hand on her stomach and she places hers on top of it.

"Does the baby move yet?" I try to think of when babies start moving, but I had been out of school too long to remember.

"Not yet, but they say anytime now. I'm nervous about it, actually."

"How come?"

"What if it feels weird? Like I know there's a baby in there, but when it starts moving? Then there's a whole person in there."

"They say most women describe it as a sort of flutter."

"So like butterflies? Because I always feel those around you."

"Wow, what a line." I tease.

"It's true! You always give me butterflies." Norah blushes and I kiss her reddening cheeks.

"You've always made me feel at peace. Like a calm I didn't know I could have until you." I admit.

"Now talk about a line." Norah teases back.

"I'm serious. I don't know how I thought you'd just be another person I knew."

"Gemma..."

"Close your eyes Norah, baby. You're exhausted." I kiss her forehead and her eyes flutter closed.

It only takes a few minutes for her silence to turn into light snores. I lean forward and whisper "I love you" into her hair. I know she can't hear me, which is good because I don't know if I'm ready to really say it yet. It hasn't been that long and I don't want to scare her. So for now, I'm happy loving her quietly.

TWENTY-FOUR

Norah

"Ugh," I grumble and throw another pair of shorts onto the pile in the corner.

"What's wrong?" Gemma walks into the room as I toss another pair.

"None of my clothes fit me," I grumble.

"Well, you are almost halfway through the pregnancy."

"So? I thought I had more time." I frown. I sit on the bed in just a shirt and my panties.

"It's good, it means the baby is growing." Gemma kneels next to me and lifts my shirt to look at my bump. I am still pretty small but there is no denying I am pregnant now. I have a round bump that is making it impossible to close any of my shorts or pants.

"I know. I guess I'll have to go shopping." I sigh.

"Why don't we go together? We can make a trip of it." Gemma places a small kiss on my bump and sits next to me on the bed.

"Really?"

"Yeah, is there a mall nearby? We can get clothes for you, some things for the nursery, and I need a few things for the bachelorette party."

"The closest mall is in the next town over."

"Okay, then let's make a day of it."

"I need something to wear to the mall though." I frown.

"Do your dresses fit you?"

"Probably." I stand up and look for a soft cotton one. Lately my skin has been more sensitive than normal. I don't want to wear anything that might be itchy or uncomfortable.

"You look beautiful in the blue one," Gemma says coming up behind me.

"I do like that one." I smile.

Pulling it out of the closet, I toss my shirt aside and slide the dress on. It's a little tight on my boobs, which is new to me, but it's not tight on my stomach. I guess this looks good. I turn to the side and the way the dress is cut, it actually highlights my little bump.

"Is it weird that I love that you're starting to show?"

"You do?"

"You just look beautiful normally, but fuck you're like glowing lately," Gemma murmurs.

She leans in to kiss my neck and I groan. I close my eyes as she presses her lips all the way up the nape of my neck.

"Okay, if you continue that, we're not going anywhere." I laugh.

"Mm, fine. Let's go then." Gemma takes my hand, and I follow her to the kitchen.

"What are you getting?"

"I'm packing you some snacks," she says, like it's obvious.

"I'm not a child. I don't need snacks." I frown.

"I'm going to say this politely, but I don't want to be caught with you when you're hungry. These are emergency snacks, just in case."

"Fine," I grumble. It isn't me, it's the pregnancy hormones that make me extra hungry and extra grumpy when I go too long without food.

Gemma kisses my cheek and I put my sneakers on by the

To Be Loved

door. Gemma likes to drive, and I'm kind of tired so I let her drive us. She puts the directions to the mall on her car's GPS and turns on the radio for some music.

"I was thinking about telling Finn's parents about the baby."

"Oh yeah?" Gemma glances at me.

"I've been afraid to tell them. I don't know how they'll react, and I didn't want to get their hopes up in case something happened. But I'm sort of in the clear now, and with all our friends knowing, I don't want them to hear it from someone else. Lovers is a small town."

"That makes sense. Are you nervous?"

"Oh, yes." I nod.

"Because you think they might react badly?" she guesses.

"I just don't know how they'll react. Finn was quite private, so it's not like they know I've had our embryos sitting around all this time. I can't just blurt out I'm pregnant or they'll think it's someone random."

"I'm sure if you explain it to them, they'll understand. I can't see them being upset considering you're carrying their grandchild. You've said they're both very kind and open, so maybe they'll be happy to have a chance to have a connection to Finn just like you wanted."

"That does make sense."

"It might also bring up the question of if I'm seeing anyone."

"I think I know what you're asking."

"You do?"

"Norah, under no circumstances are you required to tell them about me. If you want to, sure. But there's no pressure either way. In your own time, you can tell them about us."

"Really?"

"Of course. They're Finn's parents, they're not yours or our friends or something."

"That's true." We decided together that we would tell the rest of our friends about us after the wedding.

"Just do whatever you feel is best for you. I'll support you either way." She smiles.

I grab her hand that's not on the wheel and squeeze it tightly. I'm still nervous as heck to tell Finn's parents about the baby, but at least I know that, no matter what, I'll have Gemma on my side.

"We should get one of those warm pretzels when we get to the mall," Gemma says.

"Um, yes please. And a big lemonade."

"Ooo yes, that's like my favorite part of going to the mall." She laughs.

Thirty-two minutes later, we pull into the mall parking lot. It's pretty full for a weekday, but it's the summertime and the only mall within an hour of a few small towns. Gemma looks at the directory in the middle of the mall and then leads us to the maternity stores. I like shopping, but shopping for clothes that would only fit me for a few months seems pointless. I do need stuff to wear to work and pants that won't pop open when I breathe. Gemma picks out a few dresses for me to try on, and I grab some maternity pants.

"Go try stuff on. I'll hold your purse." Gemma leads me to the dressing room and takes a seat on the bench nearby.

I try everything on, which is more exhausting that I thought it would be. I like everything except one of the dresses is too short. I pay for everything and then we go looking for a hot pretzel. I can smell them, so I follow my nose, which makes me feel like a hound dog. The pretzel place is right next to a baby store, so we get two pretzels and one lemonade to share and go in the store.

"Everything is so tiny." Gemma holds up little onesies and makes an awe face.

"It would be easier to pick things out if we knew the baby's gender," I tease.

"Norah, let's be real, you're not picking things based on gender. It's 2024, you're going to pick clothes based on cuteness," Gemma points out. I hate that she's right. Boy or girl, they'll have too many clothes to choose from in all colors.

"Oh my goodness, you have to get this." Gemma holds up a little onesie with a book on it that says, 'future reader'.

"Holy crap, that's so cute." I take it from her and hold it up.

It's so small, she's right. There's a woman nearby with a baby strapped to her chest. The baby can't be more than a few months old, just moving its little head around to see the world. That's going to be me one day soon. My hand falls to my stomach, and I don't even realize I'm crying until the tear falls.

"Whoa, Norah, baby. What's wrong?" Gemma asks, rushing to my side.

"I'm having a baby."

"I hope this isn't just occurring to you." Gemma dry laughs.

"I mean, I'm going to have a real life baby soon. What the hell was I thinking?"

"Hey, you were thinking that you've always wanted to be a mom. You want a baby, and you want a way to let Finn be a father. It's fine to be nervous, but you're going to be okay." Gemma gives me a hug and wipes my tears away.

"Thank you."

"It's okay. It's totally normal to freak out. We have at least one nervous mother in the ER each week worried about this stuff."

"Really?"

"Oh, yeah. One woman threatened to camp out there until she gave birth. Norah, I was the one who told her she was pregnant. She wanted to camp out there for months."

"Well, at least I'm not that bad." I laugh.

"Exactly, big picture."

I walk around the rest of the store, picking out some things for the baby. We get the reader shirt and a few other onesies that have silly phrases on them. I'm convinced they're more for the parents to read and laugh. Gemma gives me the lemonade to finish, which makes me have to pee exactly four times before we leave the mall.

While we're on our way home, I spot an indie bookstore and Gemma pulls into the parking lot without me asking. She said she wasn't going to deny me a bookstore date. We walk around the bookstore, looking at the first editions they have and the special editions of new books. Gemma holds my purse again, claiming it's too heavy for me. I think she just likes holding things for me.

"Have you gotten the baby any books yet?" Gemma asks, and I stop short.

"No." I can't believe I haven't thought to grab a book for the baby.

"That's surprising. We should see what they have." Gemma leads me to the kids' section in the back of the store.

I look for my favorite childhood book, *The Runaway Bunny*. It's about this little bunny who tells his mom he's going to run away, and then the mother says no matter what or where he is, she'll always find him. It's a cute story that my mom used to read to me when I was a kid. I find a paperback edition on the shelf, and I know it's a sign to buy it. Gemma's looking through the kids' books too, and I wonder aloud what her favorite kids' book is.

"I always had a soft spot for *Chrysanthemum*."

"I don't know that one." I frown.

"It's about a girl who I think is a bunny, who hates her name because she gets made fun of for it being so long. And being named after a flower. Then she learns to love it and everyone else wants a unique name too," she explains. "Here it is."

Gemma holds up the yellow book; it looks sweet.

"Would it be okay if I got it for the baby?"

"Of course, I think the baby can never have enough books." I smile.

"Truer words have never been said." Gemma agrees.

On the way out, I spot familiar red hair. "Sutton?"

"Norah!? What are you doing here?" She gives me a hug and smiles.

"Just shopping. What about you?"

"Same here, I was at the mall with some friends and wanted to check this place out."

"We went to the mall too. Gemma, this is my friend and co-worker, Sutton. Sutton, this is my girlfriend, Gemma." It's the first time I'm saying it aloud, and I notice how natural it sounds on my tongue.

"Girlfriend?! Wow. Okay, so that's what you've been hiding." She laughs. "*SO* nice to meet you, Gemma."

"Pleasure is mine, I've heard good things."

"Is someone having a baby shower?" Sutton eyes the kids' books.

"Yup, old college friend of mine. We're just getting some of our favorites." Gemma quickly lies for me. One secret was enough to share today. I'll tell Sutton soon, but I need to tell Mama and Papa Perry first.

"Well, I should get going, but I'll see you at work. And it was nice meeting you, Gemma." Sutton smiles and heads out the door.

I take Gemma's hand as we pay for both books and relax a little. Maybe telling people Gemma is my girlfriend isn't as scary as I thought it might be.

Epilogue I

NORAH

"Norah?! What a lovely surprise," Finn's dad, Papa Perry, answers the door with a smile.

"Hi Jerry." I smile. He's the spitting image of Finn and what I always assumed Finn would look like when he's older.

"Babe! We have a guest; our daughter is here," he calls out to Mama Perry. My heart warms when he calls me his daughter and not daughter-in-law.

"Norah! Oh dear, what a nice surprise." She's wearing an apron that's covered in cows but not an actual speck of food on it.

"I hope it's okay I stopped by."

"Of course, come on in. We were just making some apple pie, it should be done in about ten minutes." Mama Perry smiles.

I kick off my shoes by the front door and follow them into the kitchen. Papa Perry's holding a cold beer and takes a seat across from me.

"Want one?" He tilts the beer toward me, and I shake my head. Although I wish I could have one right about now. No one prepares you for telling your parents-in-law you're pregnant with their dead son's baby.

"So, I was hoping I could talk to you both about something. Sort of important." I clear my throat.

"Of course." Papa Perry looks at me, and I wait for Mama Perry to take a seat. They hold hands on the table, and I can tell they're anxious, so I might as well spit it out.

"I have some news, some big news. And I want you to hear me first before you react."

"Okay." They both nod.

"I'm pregnant. And it's Finn's. It's your grand baby."

They both give me a vacant stare. I don't blame them. But it's Papa Perry who's first to speak.

"Not that we don't, uh, believe you dear, but I think I'm a little old and a little lost on how that's possible."

"Finn and I were trying to have a baby when he passed. We had embryos saved, so about four-ish months ago, I was artificially inseminated at the doctor's office. So, Finn and I are having a baby." I pull out the most recent sonogram and place it on the table near them.

Mama Perry gasps when she sees it and picks it up. She takes her glasses off her neck and puts them on the bridge of her nose. Papa Perry looks at her and then the sonogram.

"I know this is probably shocking. Finn and I were keeping things private when he was alive. And I didn't have any intention of using it without him. But I honestly couldn't imagine having anyone else's baby," I add.

"Oh my goodness, we're having a grand baby!" Mama Perry bursts out of her seat and wraps her arms around me. I relax in her cozy and warm arms.

"We really are, huh?" Papa Perry looks the photo over.

"I was worried you might be upset. I'm almost halfway through the pregnancy. But I wanted to be sure that everything was okay with the baby."

"Is it?" She looks at me nervously.

"It is. Everything is on track. I'm due in January, and the baby is measuring perfectly."

To Be Loved

"That's amazing." She sighs a breath of relief.

The timer dings, and she jumps up to take out her pie.

"Finn would've loved to be a father. I'm sorry we're not getting to see that, but I'm glad we get to see you have our grandchild and be a part of their life." Papa Perry smiles at me.

"Of course, it's so important to me that this baby knows about Finn and has a close relationship with you both."

"We're so glad you came to tell us, dear." Mama Perry smiles.

"And you thought she was seeing someone," Papa Perry teases.

"Actually…" I wasn't sure if I was going to bring this up today, but since there is an opening.

"I knew it! Pay up Jerry!" Mama hits his shoulder playfully.

"You are seeing someone then?" He raises an eyebrow.

"This next part might be even harder, but yes. I've been seeing someone for about a month now, and I really like them. We're still getting to know each other, but I can see it being something special."

"That's lovely, dear, we just want you to be happy. Finn would've wanted that too." She smiles.

"It's actually a woman I'm seeing." I wince. I don't know how they might take something like this.

"Oh." They both look at me in surprise. "Does that mean you're…"

"It means I loved Finn and now I like this woman, Gemma. It doesn't negate my marriage, I think I just fall for the person regardless of gender," I explain.

"Well, as long as she makes you happy." Mama Perry smiles and reaches for my hand.

"Really?" I can't help it; a few loose tears fall down my cheeks with no warning.

"Of course, oh my goodness, dear." Mama Perry jumps up to hug me again. "Is it surprising? Yes, to both news. But that's okay, we just want you to be happy. Finn would be so happy knowing you're having his baby and so are we. Whoever you end up with, we just want them to make you and this baby happy." She holds my face as she talks to me.

"Okay." I wipe my tears, and she pulls me in for a tight hug.

"We love you, darlin', and you're always family to us." Papa Perry stands, joining in the group hug.

I don't know why I was so nervous to tell them. Of course, they would be accepting and happy. They raised Finn, and he was one of the best people I've ever known. He was just like his parents, and I'm so glad they're going to get to see this baby raised close by.

"Let's have some pie, and you can tell us all about how you're feeling." Mama Perry breaks the hug and grabs some plates.

We all sit around the table and talk about the baby. I tell them about the new apartment and promise to have them over once the place is set up. Right now, it's still all open boxes and an unfinished nursery. I think they're relieved to hear I have a permanent place in Lovers again. I mean, I'm locked into my lease for at least a year, and I can't imagine going anywhere else. I tell them how the baby kicks now and moves around my stomach. It's a surreal feeling the baby float around in there. I'm so glad Gemma was there the first time it happened.

"Promise you'll come around, and if you need anything for you or the baby, just give us a call. We're happy to do anything we can," Mama Perry says as I stand by the front door.

"I promise. Once the nursery is done, I'll have you both over to see it too." I smile.

She gives me one last hug and I head for the car. I look at the time on my dash and smile. Gemma should be home from work by the time I get home. We both pull into the driveway at the same time, and Gemma unlocks the door for us. The second we're inside, I wrap my arms around her neck and kiss her.

"I take it your day went well?" She smiles.

"They're so happy. I told them about everything. The baby and you!" I say excitedly.

"Really?" Her eyes light up.

"Yeah! It just kind of came out, and they were so supportive of everything," I explain.

"That's so great. I know how worried you were about this." She kisses my cheeks and then my lips.

"Did you have dinner yet?" I ask.

"I did, actually. I grabbed food on the way home because I was starving. Did you eat?"

"Just some apple pie, but I think I want a peanut butter and jelly for dinner."

"Mmm, you want me to make it?"

"No, that's okay. I know you like to shower when you come home. Why don't you go relax, and I'll meet you in the spare room? I just downloaded a new book I wanna read." I smile.

"Sounds perfect." Gemma kisses my forehead and heads for her room.

I make my sandwich, grab my reading stuff from my room, and put it in the spare room. Then I pee and decide to grab Gemma a glass of wine. I place it on the table in the spare room and light one of the scented candles. It's one of the ones I like that aren't too strong of a scent. I relax in my usual spot and eat my sandwich with one hand while using the other to turn the pages on my Kindle. I'm all snuggled up in my blanket when Gemma comes in the room.

Her hair is wet in a messy bun on top of her head, and she's in pajamas. She's holding a blanket and her kindle in her hands. I smile. God, she's so beautiful without even trying.

"Wow, you brought me wine? Mmm." She takes a sip and sits down next to me.

I make a little more room for her as she gets comfortable. She takes a sip of her wine and then turns on her Kindle. We're both quiet as we read. It's my favorite time of day because we don't do this every night, but when we do, it's so intimate. Her body next to mine, both of us reading, usually romances. I usually sip tea while she drinks her wine. This is how I got to know her. I love that our love of books is what brought us together.

The baby kicks lightly, and I press my palm to my stomach. Whenever I'm still, the baby likes to kick. As if to say, *hi mom, I'm in here!* It's one of my favorite things. At night before bed, Gemma and I tell the baby about our day and talk to it. They say it's good for the baby to recognize its parents' voices once they're out of the womb. I know Gemma and I are taking things slow, but I have no doubt in my mind that she's trying to be this baby's parent. In no way is she trying to replace Finn, but I know she wants this baby almost as much as she wants me.

"Is the baby kicking?" Gemma looks at my belly.

"Yeah, they're active tonight." I smile.

Gemma puts down her Kindle and places her hand on my belly. "Hi baby."

Thump. Thump. Thump.

It's safe to say this baby likes Gemma too. It probably feels how I feel around Gemma and knows this is someone safe we can trust. The baby often kicks more when she's talking or is just around. Gemma keeps her hand steady on my belly and smiles.

"I love when you do that."

"I love getting to feel them grow."

Gemma kisses me lightly and I blush. She has this effect on me that made my whole body feel like Jell-O when she kisses me. The baby kicks even harder this time, and we both laugh.

"Okay, the baby wants a kiss too." Gemma slides my T-shirt over my belly and kisses my skin. She places soft kisses all over it. The baby kicks, and I smile.

It's too easy to fall in love with her. I know it hasn't been that long, but I'm a firm believer in *when you know, you know.* Plus, life is short, and you never know what might happen. I am falling in love with Gemma, and soon, I'll have the confidence to tell her. Gemma rests her head on my chest and props her Kindle on my belly. We both go back to reading, me softly rubbing her shoulders. Gemma keeps one hand on my belly. I've never been more relaxed than in this moment.

Epilogue II

GEMMA

I know I need to get Norah out of the house today so Alana and Ryleigh can set up for the gender reveal. It's proving harder than I anticipated because Norah woke up sleepier than usual. It's already eleven, and we're only getting out of bed now. Norah's cuddling on my chest, and I'm wondering how I can convince her to leave the house with me before noon.

"Do you wanna go out for breakfast?" I ask Norah.

"Hmm, wouldn't we have to leave soon though?"

"Yeah, but it might be worth it. The pancakes, the sausages, the bacon."

"I don't know. Maybe we can just wait until lunch."

"What if we have a shower together and then go for breakfast?"

"Mmm, that sounds good, but I'm honestly still spent from last night."

"Norah, baby, why don't you let me take you out for breakfast. I'm starving."

"If you really want to, I guess we can." Norah groans.

"I do!" I say, probably a bit too excitedly because Norah looks at me curiously.

I hop out of bed and pull out the dress I've set aside for the party.

"A dress? I don't think I've ever seen you in a dress." Norah muses from the bed. I don't blame her, I am more of a "dresses are for special occasions" kind of gal.

"I think it would be nice if we got dressed up for once."

"Okay." Norah yawns and sits up in bed.

"Why don't I go pick a dress for you?"

"Are you in a rush or something?"

"Nope! Just hungry, that's all," I lie. I didn't think it would be this hard to get her out of the house.

I race to her room and pick out her white sundress we bought recently. It's new, and she looks beautiful in it; plus, it highlights her bump. Now that everyone knows about the pregnancy, there's no need to hide it. I head back to my room where Norah's in the bathroom. I change into the blue dress and put on just a bit of makeup.

"Here's your dress, baby." I knock lightly on the door and slide it on the doorknob.

Five minutes later, Norah is dressed and I'm rushing her out the front door. We take my car to the diner just outside of town. I'm so nervous about today. I can barely think about food, but I know I need to eat something. Norah orders French toast with lots of berries and a side of bacon. I order some pancakes and hash browns.

"Are you okay? You seem fidgety for some reason." Norah raises an eyebrow.

"I'm okay. Just hungry," I lie.

"This place is nice. I haven't been here since I was a kid." Norah smiles.

"Alana recommended it as a good brunch place."

"Makes sense. Alana is a sucker for unlimited mimosas." Norah laughs.

"One time in college, she drank so many that they tried to cut her off, but she argued that it's called unlimited for a reason and made them bring her two more. Of course, then she puked once we got outside, but hey at least it was in the bushes."

"Oh, my goodness. One time I drank so much I slept in the wrong dorm room. I woke up so confused with a girl waking me up telling me I was in her bed. My friends called me Goldie Locks for the next year," Norah says.

The waiter brings us our food, and it's delicious. I'm hungry at first, but seeing everything in front of me makes my stomach growl. I share my hash browns with Norah, and she gives me a piece of bacon.

"We're officially one of those cheesy couples," I joke as I feed her a piece of my pancakes off my fork.

"Yes, but like, the really cute cheesy couples," she insists.

"For sure," I agree.

After brunch, I check my phone while Norah's in the bathroom. For once, I'm thankful for how often she pees. Alana and Ryleigh give me the go ahead that everything's ready, and it's okay for us to come back. I'm relieved and relax a little. The drive back seems quicker than going, but maybe it's because I'm excited about today. I love the chance to spoil Norah, and today is all about her.

"Wanna go in and take a nap?" Norah looks at me expectantly. Normally I'd say yes, hands down.

"Uh, why don't we get a snack first?" I hope that, despite the fact that we just ate, she might want some cherries.

"Mm, okay." She nods.

I follow her to the kitchen, and then realize I need a way to get her to come outside with me.

"Come with me a minute?" I don't wait for an answer and pull her with me.

"Why are we going outside? Can't we just go lie down? I'm so ready for a nap—"

"Surprise!" Everyone jumps out and yells at once.

"Oh, you guys! I said I didn't want anything big." There goes my tears. Apparently I'm a happy crier these days too.

"This isn't big, I had to talk Alana down from the 3-tier cake she wanted," Ryleigh teases.

"Hey! Babies are a big deal! I just wanted to spoil the little nugget." Alana smiles.

"Are you going to introduce me? Or I can go hide out in my room if I'm not invited," Gemma teases.

"Everyone, this is Gemma." I smile. "She's Alana's maid of honor and has been spending the summer here."

"Before you take a seat, mama, you have to pop the balloon and tell us what you're having." Ryleigh instructs.

"Okay, I'm so nervous." I walk over to the cake table where Ryleigh is untangling a huge black balloon.

Heather picks up her camera and starts taking photos of me.

"Okay, ready?" I'm handed a pin, and I close my eyes before poking the ballon. Out bursts bright pink confetti all over her and the ground.

"Yes!" Heather exclaims loudly, and everyone laughs.

"Oh, my goodness!" I smile, and Gemma is there to hug me first. I wrap my arms around Gemma's neck, and Gemma holds me tightly. I almost forget where we are and kiss her too. But at the last moment, I let go and start hugging everyone else.

Ryleigh leads me to sit at the table where there's a huge white cake. Inside, it has pink cake. Gemma can't help but wait on me, bringing me water from in the house.

"Thank you, guys, for being here with me. It means a lot to have your support through this pregnancy." I smile.

Alana, Gemma, Kim, Heather, and Ryleigh are all happily eating the cake and talking about this summer. As I look around, I notice everyone is dressed in pink or blue. Except Ryleigh—but she's the only one who knew the gender of the baby. I place my hand on my belly, and the baby kicks as I eat the sugary cake.

"Is the baby kicking yet?" Alana asks.

"Yeah, usually when I'm sitting down. So she might start soon if you want to feel." I smile.

Alana all but jumps out of her seat to stand next to my belly. I take her hand and place it on my stomach near where she usually kicks. I poke my belly in a different spot and then, *thump, thump,* she kicks for Alana.

"Holy crap! That's so awesome!" Alana pulls back her hand in amazement.

Most of my friends take turns feeling the baby kick. I open all the presents they give me even though I tell them it's totally unnecessary. It's a bunch of cute baby clothes, gender neutral and things they assume I'll need. I'm the first of us to have a baby, so they're guessing based on google searches ,and provided gift receipt's.

"Have you thought of any names yet?" Heather asks.

"Not really. I wasn't sure if it was a boy or a girl, and I'm honestly still wrapping my head around this in general," I admit.

"I'm surprised you don't have names picked out from when you were a kid or something," Gemma jokes.

"Oh my goodness! Remember when we were kids?!" Alana squeals.

"Norah would always make us play pregnant and put a baby in our shirt. She had these totally unique names for the babies too!" Kim smiles.

"Do you remember them?" Ryleigh asks.

"I think one was like Theodora or Holland. I always wanted princess names for the baby, I think I thought it was going to marry royalty." I laugh.

"Hey, there's still time." Kim winks.

I tense, but it's not her fault. It's weird that my friends don't know about Gemma and I, but they'll know soon enough. Alana's wedding is less than two weeks away, and after that, we'll be free to tell everyone. I'm definitely counting down the days. I might get on the alter and let everyone know that Gemma is mine.

Okay, I definitely will *not* do that, but God, I want to.

BONUS EPILOGUE

NORAH

Kim calls Wrenn and Ryleigh on the phone because Alana looks like she's going to scream at them if she does. Kim says they're on their way and they overslept, which makes me put a glass of champagne in Alana's hand.

"I know it feels like everything that can go wrong is going wrong. I promise there is a bright side to today. Weddings never go according to plan, and it will be okay." I assure Alana, but she doesn't look convinced.

"Finally! Where were you two!?" Alana scowls when Wrenn and Ryleigh arrive at the bridal suite twenty minutes later. Gemma grabs me a virgin mimosa, a champagne glass of orange juice, and I sip it.

"It's my fault. I was supposed to set the alarm and forgot." Wrenn says.

"Ugh, fine. Well, you're here now." Alana sighs. "We're doing makeup, then hair, and then getting dressed."

"Okay." We both nod and slide into the chairs in front of the mirrors.

"Do you want a mimosa?" I ask when Ryleigh's done with her makeup.

"I'd love one." Ryleigh smiles.

"Wrenn? You want one?" I ask.

"Yes, please, if you don't mind." Wrenn smiles. I nod and walk to the other side of the room to grab the drinks.

"Here you are." I hand them two glasses.

"Shit, you make 'em strong." Wrenn gasps after taking a sip.

"You're both drinking for me tonight." Norah laughs.

"Got it, boss."

Alana is pacing around the room with her hair half done and staring at her phone.

"Is she okay?" Ryleigh whispers to me.

"I don't know. She's been on edge all morning." I frown.

"I'll check on her." Wrenn says. "Excuse me." She tells the hairdresser.

We watch as Wrenn walks over to Alana and tries talking to her. We can't hear what she's saying, but based on the facial expressions, it doesn't look like it's going well. I walk over and hand Alana a tissue because she looks like she's about to cry, and I don't want her to mess up her makeup.

"I just don't know if I can do this," Alana admits.

"Like the wedding or the marriage?" Wrenn asks.

"Both. All of it." Alana looks at us, but I'm not sure what we're supposed to say.

"Don't worry, you're just getting some pre wedding jitters. They'll go away." Wrenn is holding another tissue to Alana when Heather walks into the suite.

"What's going on?" Heather whispers.

"Alana's having some second thoughts." I whisper back.

"I just know I love him, but how am I supposed to be sure he's the *one*?" Alana cries. One hand has a Kleenex and the other holding onto a long-stemmed champagne glass.

"Can you tell her something encouraging? Were you nervous on your wedding day?" Heather looks at me for help. I get why I'd be the obvious choice. I was the only one who'd been married before.

I shake my head. "I wasn't nervous at all. I was sure about Finn."

We both exchange a worried glance, but before we can say anything, the wedding hair and makeup team walks in.

"Ready?" One of the women smile.

Heather and I are whisked into a chair and told to sit still. I pull my hair out of its bun and Alana, Wrenn and Ryleigh leave the suite. I was worried about her. I mean, we all were. I couldn't imagine the pressure she's been under with all the wedding preparations on her own. I had Finn and his family helping me with mine, and it was still stressful. Gemma sits down next to me and takes my hand only for a second. It was so hard to forget to not be romantic with her. A lot of our touches and looks were involuntary at this point.

"Is she going to be okay?" Heather asks me. Wrenn's back shortly after, but Alana and Wrenn are still gone.

"I don't know. I've never seen her this nervous." Gemma adds from my other side.

"Do you think we should get her mom?" Kim asks.

"No, she was just as nervous about this wedding going off without a hitch. I don't know if she can handle it if something goes wrong." Gemma explains.

"Well, I guess all we can do is get ready, then." Heather frowns. The woman starts working on my hair and I try to relax a bit. Heather tells us about Sage, the woman she's been seeing and is bringing today as her date. I get a little jealous. I can't brag about Gemma today.

"What happened?" Ryleigh whispers as Wrenn comes back alone.

"I have no clue. All I asked was if she was okay. She started telling me all the things that went wrong and then she said she was going for a walk, alone." Wrenn explains.

"Maybe it's just wedding nerves, but I don't remember you like this." Ryleigh looks at me.

"Everyone's different, but no. On my wedding day, I felt

calm, like I was finally going to be with the love of my life." I smile and absentmindedly place a hand on my belly.

"How long until the wedding?" Wrenn asks.

"About an hour. But it takes at least fifteen minutes to get her dress and veil on. Plus, her hair isn't done." I say anxiously, looking at my phone.

"Give her ten minutes, then someone will go looking for her." Ryleigh decides.

Gemma asks for some help to zip her dress, so I stand up to help her. My hair and makeup were done, so all I needed was to get dressed. I want to press kisses along Gemma's back, but my friends are all around us, so I don't.

"Do you think Alana's okay?" I look at Gemma, concerned.

"I don't know. I've never seen her like this," she admits.

"I haven't either. It's been more than ten minutes. I think I'm going to look for her." Gemma decides.

"Do you want me to come with?"

"No, you stay here and relax. I'm sure she's around somewhere and I don't want you using all your energy before the day even starts." Gemma smiles.

"Okay. Good luck." I whisper.

"You guys dressed?" I knock on the door to Wrenn and Ryleigh's suite. I figure I should let them know someone is going to look for Alana.

"I am!"

"Gemma's going to look for Alana, okay?"

"Okay!" they call through the door.

I help Kim get dressed and then I put on my own dress. One of my friends zip me up and I snap a few selfies with them but I was nervous. Gemma had been gone almost a half an hour now, and the wedding was starting soon. Where the hell was Alana? It's not like we called her. She left her phone here. Finally Gemma comes back to the room, but she looks grimly at us.

"Uh, I don't know how to say this. But I can't find Alana." Gemma says quietly.

"What?!" I gasp.

"What do you mean?" Heather asks.

Everyone starts asking about different places Gemma checked and did she forget about this or that place? But I know what's happening, Alana was running away from the wedding. All the warning signs have been here, and I thought it was just in my head. She and Will had not been getting along and she was so stressed. That wasn't how someone should be on their wedding day.

"What the fuck do we even do?" Wrenn says.

"Did anyone check on Will? Maybe she went to talk to him?" I suggest. It was my last ditch effort at attempting to see if she didn't run.

"I didn't want to worry him, but I can go check with him right now." Gemma nods.

"I'll come with you." Kim adds.

They disappear and the rest of us are quiet. I look at Alana's stuff on her phone. It's hidden in the bottom of her purse, with a million missed calls from everyone. There's no way to unlock it, so I don't have any clue to where she might have gone.

"She doesn't have her phone, so it's not like she could've gotten far." I say aloud.

"I wish she had it because then one of us could track her." Heather sighs.

I place a hand on my belly and the baby kicks lightly. She can probably feel my anxiety and I don't blame her. I quietly will her to calm down. Doing a few deep breaths for my own sake. Gemma comes back and she and Kim explain that Will hasn't seen Alana at all today.

"Are you okay?" Gemma pulls me aside to check on me.

"I feel bad. I saw the warning signs, and I thought she was just a nervous and stressed bride."

"I saw them too, but I thought it was just Will being Will." Gemma sighs.

Wrenn decides to go tell their mom about Alana. Maybe

she'd know where she was and would be able to help out. Ryleigh tagged along with her, and I plopped on the couch with another glass of orange juice.

"Why don't we go for a little walk?" Gemma suggests. I nod and follow her, leaving my juice behind.

Once we're down the hallway and alone, Gemma takes my hand in hers. It eases some of my anxiety just to be in her hands again. We reach the end of the hallway and she leads me to a balcony overlooking the water. The Lovers Lighthouse is small in the distance.

"Even if she did run away from the wedding, it's not like we won't find her. She probably just needs some space." Gemma reassures me.

"You're probably right." I nod.

"Are you thinking about your wedding day today?"

"Not really. Marrying Finn wasn't like this at all. I felt this overwhelming sense of calmness and ease. We couldn't even spend the night before our wedding apart because I was going to miss him too much. He snuck into my dressing room before I put on my dress just to see me. When it's the right person, it's not complicated. It was easy and simple." I smile.

"That's how I feel about you." Gemma says quietly.

"I feel that about you, too." I admit.

"Does that scare you?" Gemma asks.

"Oh, yes." I feel the tears welling in my eyes. But I can't stop them from overflowing. Just before they do, Gemma catches them with her hand.

"It's okay, one day it won't feel so scary to be loved by me," Gemma says softly. Her words aren't lost on me. But instead of saying anything, I kiss her. My emotions taking over.

Acknowledgments

Maybe this is my way of working through my grief. It's funny, this is the second book this year that I've written about a side character who's passed on. I plotted both of those books early into 2024 WAY before I knew anything going on in my personal life. Maybe somehow I knew I'd need a healthy way to work through my grief. Knowing someone you love is dying can be just as hard as losing someone. In a way, writing has always been healing for me. It's always been a way for me to see things in a new light. I hope that reading Norah and Gemma's story was good for you.

Thank you to my little bear who's not so little anymore. He recently told me he'd like to have my job, I was surprised to hear this, so I said really? He then asked what my job is, I told him I'm an author I write books. He tells me he wants to do that too because I don't leave the house and I stay in my pajamas all day. My four year old roasted me but hey, at least he wants to be like me. Thanks for always making me laugh and being my little light.

Thank you to my writing friends who kept pushing me with sprints, late night chats and annoying me asking me if I've hit my word count yet. You're definitely part of why I didn't give up on this.

Thank you to my family for everything you do and believing in me.

Thank you to my readers! If not for you, I wouldn't be doing this full time and that's not something I take lightly. Thank you to anyone who's picked up this book or any of the others in this series. I hope you keep reading.

Also by Shannon O'Connor

SEASONS OF SEASIDE SERIES

(each book can be read as a standalone)

Only for the Summer

Only for Convenience

Only for the Holidays

Only to Save You

Seasons of Seaside: The Complete Collection

LIGHTHOUSE LOVERS

Tour of Love

Hate to Love You

To Be Loved

Inn Love

Love, Unexpected

ETERNAL PORT VALLEY SERIES

Unexpected Departure

Unexpected Days

Eternal Port Valley: The Complete Collection

STANDALONES

Electric Love

Butterflies in Paris

All's Fair in Love & Vegas

Fumbling into You

Doll Face

Poolside Love

Eras of Us

HOLIDAY STANDALONES

Tangled Up In You

THE HOLIDAYS WITH YOU

(each book can be read as a standalone)

I Saw Mommy Kissing the Nanny

Lucky to be Yours

The Only Reason

Ugly Sweater Christmas

POETRY

For Always

Holding on to Nothing

Say it Everyday

Midnights in a Mustang

Five More Minutes

When Lust Was Enough

Isolation

All of Me

Lost Moments

Cosmic

Goodbye Lovers

About the Author

Shannon O'Connor is a twenty something, bisexual, self published author of several poetry books and counting. She released her debut contemporary romance novel, *Electric Love* in 2021. O'Connor is continuously working on new poetry projects, book reviews, and more, while also diving into motherhood. When she's not reading or writing she can be found watching Disney movies with her son where they reside in New York. She is currently a full time mom and full time author.

She sometimes writes as S O'Connor for MF romances and as Shannon Renee for Poly romances.

Heat. Heart. & HEA's.

Check out more work & updates on:
Facebook Group: https://www.facebook.com/groups/shanssquad

Website: https://shanoconnor.com

- facebook.com/AuthorShanOConnor
- instagram.com/authorshannonoconnor
- bookbub.com/authors/shannon-o-connor
- pinterest.com/Shannonoconnor1498
- threads.net/@authorshannonoconnor

Printed in Great Britain
by Amazon